Baltimore Catechism:

A
Year
of
Confirmation

John T. Hourihan Jr.

Aster Press
Blue Fortune Enterprises, LLC

BALTIMORE CATECHISM: YEAR OF CONFIRMATION

For information contact :
Blue Fortune Enterprises, LLC
Aster Press
P.O. Box 554
Yorktown, VA 23690
http://blue-fortune.com

Book and Cover design by Blue Fortune Enterprises, LLC

ISBN: 978-1-948979-70-2

First Edition: September 2021

This book is a gem. This story of a young Irish boy trying to understand the seeming difference between religion and reality is laugh out loud funny. But you don't have to be Irish or Catholic to enjoy this nostalgic journey into the past as he struggles to do the right thing.

Patti Gaustad Procopi, author of *Please… Tell Me More*

As a fellow writer of semi-autobiographic fiction, I applaud John Hourihan's new book, *Baltimore Catechism*. Told with the innocence of childhood and the tongue-in cheek irony of adulthood, the book brings out the conflict between religion and reality. Through the eyes of a young Irish-American boy, the book explores what it means to be religious. The author's sardonic whit, coupled with his poignant visual, auditory and olfactory images of people, places and events, makes the book an enticing read. This book is a paean to our common humanity and to what is good in all of us.

Christian Pascale, author of *Memories Are The Stories We Tell Ourselves* and *Windows of Heaven*.

Dedication

This book is dedicated to my brothers and sisters Patricia,
Diane, Nancy, Sheila, Dennis and Cornelius.
It is amazing what we survived.
And to my classmates with whom I shared so much.

The seven gifts of the Holy Spirit at Confirmation are knowledge, understanding, wisdom, counsel, fortitude, piety, and fear of the Lord.

Chapter One
Paradise Lost
July

Sometimes the cold of deep winter doesn't fully disappear with spring.

Instead, a piece of it hides in your soul like a pocket of unmeltable ice. It is carried silently until it surfaces unexpectedly from time to time. A piece of my heart froze on an early spring day when I was nine years old. The bank had taken my family's home, and the nine of us were forced to leave.

I lost my faith in people, and being Irish-Catholic, I knew that when I died, there would be some serious questions for God.

I had lived in my home on Purchase Street, four miles

from town and a quarter mile down the dirt and gravel driveway, since my fourth birthday. I knew the paths in the woods, the lake for fishing and ice skating, and the granite quarry where the bigger kids swam. I knew the stone wall where I used to sit and wait for my father to come home from work at the shoe shop. My friends, Spike, Peter, Danny, Robbie, and Linda all lived here nearly within spitting distance of my house. Of course, instead of spitting, if we wanted the others to come out, we shouted a high-pitched, pre-pubescent scream, *ee-oo-eet* and everyone came to play. It was heaven. We all had a spiritual side at school and church and a worldly side at home. For instance, I'd received a spiritual baptism at the church before I could talk, but my worldly baptism happened on my fourth birthday when we moved here. My first worldly communion occurred a short time later when I was allowed to go out into the woods by myself.

I had eaten 6,570 meals in that kitchen; climbed into the warmth of my bed 2,190 times; attended 42 family birthdays; six Christmases, Easters, and Halloweens. I had sat in the big room and listened to Red Sox games with my father somewhere near 700 times, and I had been lost blueberry picking out by the high tension wires and followed the dog home just once.

That is, incidentally, the same number of times my

family got evicted from our home by a money-grubbing bank.

Just once.

Since I was a devout St. Mary's Catholic boy, raised in part by the Sisters of the order of St. Joseph, I supposed this was payback from the bankers for Jesus having thrown them out of the temple. That holy ejection was why sometimes when I walked by the bank I looked up into the sun and winked at God, a quick thank you.

Back then, in the mid-fifties, if a homeowner missed a payment or two, that might result in dire consequences. The bank did whatever it wanted. This time, someone wanted to make money. My family owned a falling-down, cedar-shingled, five-room house, a barn, and six acres of land up the North Purchase, halfway to Hopkinton, deep in the New England woods. The bank took it all for a few missed payments shortly after my father had lost his job at the shoe shop.

One day, we got a notice from the sheriff that said we were being given two weeks to move out. I never saw the sheriff. He just showed up in the early morning darkness and secretly left his note. We didn't even see it until the sun came up. I shoved the door open, headed out with a box of Kix to go across the yard by the barn to get some raspberries for breakfast when I saw the notice. I untaped it from the door and brought it to my mother. I couldn't understand this. I mean, this was our home. What, I thought, did the sheriff have to do with it? Mum, Sweet Genevieve to most people, stared at it and put it down on the kitchen table silently and sat down to drink her tea. As she drank, she read. Until that moment, I always thought of the sheriff as a good guy. In my world of good guys and bad guys, the sheriff dressed in a white hat and wore a five-point star for a badge. His job entailed arresting bad guys and protecting kids and women from horrible things. Sheriffs had names like Earp, Garrett, Hickock and John "Liver-Eating" Johnson of the Indian Territories. My older cousin Sean told me this last one, so I'm not sure he was real, but I liked the name, so I remembered it. Now, with this typed-out notice signed by the sheriff and tacked to our door, I knew that this thing about lawmen all being good guys was what my mother called "chicken feathers." No good guy would put a notice on the door of a woman raising seven kids on what my father brought home from work, after stopping first at the Brass Rail, and tell her to get out. He certainly couldn't have been a Catholic. Catholics knew a sin when we saw one. We didn't always avoid them. We just knew they were wrong. We might commit a sin, but a Catholic would never sign his name to it and tack it to someone's door. We mostly did our sinning anonymously.

My family moved downtown to a three-family walk-up apartment building across from The Pine Street Baptist Church and Temple Beth Shalom. We lived on the third floor. I had been raised in St. Mary's Church and school, and I felt like I'd moved to a foreign country. I woke up early one perfectly blue, sunshine-filled day in July only a few months after the eviction, pumped up the tires on my 24-inch blue and silver American Flyer, and began pedaling up and down Pine Street. After a few times, I stopped where it met Lincoln Square, across from the Greyhound station, in front of what I had been told was Ju's Chinese laundry, and I wondered, *How can Jews be Chinese?* Then it occurred to me: of course, there must be some Chinese Jews, right? I mean, there were Catholics and Protestants all over the world, so why not Jews in China? *It must be convenient to have the temple right up the street*, I thought.

I left the laundry and passed the Electric Company with the picture of Reddy Kilowatt in the window. I thought that the mascot name was pretty clever. My father used the word "clever" to describe Japanese people. It meant they weren't really smart, but they were just below smart on the scale of intelligence. WWII had ended only ten years ago, and people in the United States still didn't want to humanize the Japanese too much. I figured if people humanized them too much, they would have to answer for putting their families into internment camps in Arizona or dropping atomic bombs on them in Japan. Saying they were "clever" kept them below us on the scale of humanity in a place where we could look down on them and excuse our own unchristian actions. It also meant the Irish could take one more step up the social ladder, in their minds.

I began to pedal onto Main Street and realized my subconscious mind had sent me on a mission. It wasn't like the missions paid for by the Bishops' Relief Fund, but like the missions of Herb Philbrick, the government agent on the TV show *I Led Three Lives*. It was about a guy who worked as a Boston advertising executive and a spy for both the FBI and the communists. My old man loved that show. I was never sure whose side he was on, especially now, after the pinnacle of capitalism swiped our home right out from under us.

I took a left in Lincoln Square, in front of the Crystal Spa, and peddled my bike the five miles to 197 Purchase Street, the home the bank stole.

I bounced down the dirt-and-gravel driveway, dropped my bike outside in front of the house, and walked off beside the barn where the blackberry bushes were. In sublime arrogance, I picked and ate a handful of the bank's berries, sitting below the bank's climbing tree, and daring someone, anyone, to try to make me stop.

I had no idea why, but I hesitated, almost afraid to go through the front door. Finally, I took a deep breath, walked shakily to the door, blessed myself with the sign of the cross, and went inside the vacant house. My mother and four sisters would never have let it get this dusty.

My footsteps echoed off the walls, and I shivered. The sheer emptiness stunned me, but there were still artifacts of my family. A green plastic army man with the gun burned off stood as an impotent guard in the corner of the mud room just inside the door. A broken fork lay on the kitchen floor, a purple, plastic barrette in the girls' room, an unopened can of Carnation condensed milk on the kitchen shelf, and a corner of a broken Melmac dinner plate. The salesman who sold it to my mother bet me it was unbreakable. He learned that nothing in my house was unbreakable, and here was the proof.

I climbed up onto the linoleum-covered counter where I had always sat when Mum made jam-filled sugar cookies, or birthday cakes with lard-and-powdered-sugar frosting, and I stuck my head inside the cupboards. They were empty except for the smell of nutmeg.

I went into the big room and sat in the corner where

we used to put the Christmas tree. And sure enough, three brown pine needles nestled in the space between two floorboards. I picked them out and held them for a few seconds between my fingers. I tried to envision past Christmases, the multi-colored lights, the ribbon candy, the hot crossed buns. I tossed the needles in vain on the floor.

In the hall, behind the radiator, sat a Valentine card I had written to Lorraine in third grade but had been too embarrassed to deliver. I tucked it into my pocket, a piece of good feelings gone by.

I fumbled through the bedrooms.

The boys' room looked huge without the wall-to-wall bed. I glanced at the corner that used to be the space under the bed where I hid when my father came home drunk.

I went out and sat on the floor in the sun porch. I laid my head back against the wall and let the sun beat on my face. Looking out through the expanse of windows in front of me, I could see the swing tree in the front yard with the truck tire hanging on a rope from the lower branch. I thought about the day, not so long ago, that I untied it and stood it up in the dirt driveway. Only an hour or so before, I had watched the circus show on TV, the Big Top, and I saw dogs jumping through hoops. An idea struck me. I had backed off the tire about twenty feet, ran fearlessly at it and dove through. The first half of my body made it fine, and then I landed. The tire flopped forward, hit me in the back of the head, and buried my face in the dirt of the driveway. I sat on the front step, pondering what I had done wrong when my Uncle Dan and Aunt Rose arrived. My aunt peered down at me as they approached.

"My God, Johnny, have you been eating dirt?" she asked.

"Don't worry," my uncle said with a smile, "You have to eat about a pound of dirt before you die."

As they passed me, and the door slammed behind them, I took him at his word and decided, "I guess I better get started."

I nearly choked to death right there trying to get a head start on the pound of dirt my uncle said I would have to eat before I died. I laughed, wondering if grown-ups knew how they sounded to kids.

Sitting in my vacant house with the sun on my face, I cried. I don't know why I cried. It wasn't about remembrance of the tire, or the dirt, or my uncle. I couldn't help it. I closed my eyes against the sun glaring in through the sun-porch windows. I thought I could smell incense burning. In the darkness behind my closed eyes, I could see him again: the scowling face, the purple robes, the closed eyes, a visiting priest shouting the names of saints, shaking me. I felt the chill of fear inside me. I had this dream often, sometimes even when I wasn't fully asleep.

I had never felt so helpless. I opened my eyes.

This had been my home most of my life, and I hadn't been able to save it against the omnipotence and cold-heartedness of "The Bank." I felt as small as any nine-year–old ever felt. I prayed to God and Superman, not knowing which was more powerful against the monsters of finance, and even that didn't help. Sometimes Superman is busy, and sometimes God says, "No."

I opened my eyes and left the house. I had a new mission to fulfill.

I biked back to Pine Street in a blur of tears and anger, threw my bike on the front lawn, bounded up the stairs to our apartment, and slammed inside the front door.

"Why did they take our house?" I demanded of my mother.

She turned from the morning dishes in the sink, wiped her hands on her apron, and asked calmly, "Have you been there?"

"Yes."

"Don't ever go back there. We don't own it anymore.

You could be arrested. Or hurt."

"Why did they take it?" I shouted again.

She sat me down at the table and poured some tea for both of us.

"They are going to build something, I think. Maybe some businesses."

We sat quietly, drinking our tea.

A song came on the radio about The Blue Water Line. I listened intently as it told of a historical train, Ole' Number Nine.

"The City Council met last night, the vote was four to three, To tear the home town depot down and build a factory."

We listened, and I found out that they were going to, *"Take old engine number nine and turn it into scrap."* It seemed to me to be such a stupid thing to do. Then the song said, *"If you can't afford a quarter, then you ought to give a dime."*

I turned to Mum. "Can we send a dime?"

She sipped, smiled, and said, "Sure. You find the address, and I'll mail them the dime."

We laughed, and she said, "You've been crying."

I didn't understand how she could have known that. I hadn't cried since halfway home, and I was sure the wind from pedaling my bike with such speed must have dried my tears pretty good. I didn't answer. No matter what happened, a Hourihan boy was not supposed to cry.

I was nearly ten years old, and I had learned that some people didn't go by the most important rule taught to me by the Sisters of St. Joseph at St. Mary's Central Catholic Grammar School. I had been told that if I forgot everything else I learned about my Catholic religion, I should remember to believe there is something larger than myself, and I should treat others the way I wanted to be treated. It was clear to me that no one would want to have their home stolen, so I did not understand how people who would not want it to happen to them would do it to someone else.

With what was about to happen to my family, though, it didn't matter.

Chapter Two
When the Rules are Wrong
August

On sunny mornings, the gray Morgan chair on our new front porch provided a dry, comfortable seat. It had become my favorite perch all summer, watching the cars go by, and the Jews and Protestants arriving to worship. On this warm, pre-breakfast August morning, I snuggled deep into the pillows and waited for the warmth of the sun to make it past the shadow of the porch roof.

It was Saturday. My newest friend, Pudge, who lived in the apartment below ours, was eleven years old. We met for the first time when his family came up to our place to visit. Both of us were quiet at first, but before long we saw that we were in the same predicament — if we didn't make friends with each other, we would have no friends here at all. We became friends that first day. Pudge's most individual attributes were he never combed his black hair, and he could sweat standing still. As usual, my friend got up later than I did on Saturdays and was just now making his way out onto the porch. Within minutes, we had gone around to the back of the house and were smoking my mother's Pall Malls under the stairs to the third floor of the tenement where I lived.

Unexpectedly, my father, a tall, handsome, black Irishman, who was called Scrapper Jack by pretty much everyone, yelled for me from the other side of the house. I hurriedly snuffed out the cigarette in the dirt, clutched the underside of a wooden stair, pulled myself up and shouted, "Whaaat?" Pudge hid the smokes under the bottom stair between the two pieces of linoleum we had put there for just this purpose. We raced around the house toward the front, and as we rounded the corner, I could see both our fathers standing beside Pudge's black family Plymouth.

"C'mon," his old man said, and the fathers climbed into the car, Scrapper Jack in the passenger seat and George, Pudge's father, behind the wheel. We scurried into the back seat, and we were off. Since both our fathers and both our mothers smoked, we never worried that they would smell the tobacco on us. We turned out to be right in that.

"Where are we going?" I asked.

"Dump," my father answered.

Pudge and I squinted at each other in confusion. "Wait a minute!" he shouted frantically. "I have my good shoes on. I need to change first." The car stopped.

"Hurry up," both men said in unison.

In a flash, we were back on the road, headed for the dump, and Pudge leaned over to tie his old, scuffed shoes. Kids of our economic status always had problems with shoes. They wore out long before we were allowed to replace them, so we found ways to extend their lives. Mine, at the moment, had a hole in the right sole, so I stuffed a piece of cardboard from the box they came out of inside. When I took off my shoe, I could see Buster Brown and Tige looking at me. I used the rest of the box to hold my baseball cards. It was strange that Pudge's left shoe had a hole in the top. How the hell he got a hole in the top, I will never know. It couldn't have worn out that way.

I had no idea why we were going to the dump, but I was pretty sure my friend had retrieved the pack of smokes, so we would probably get lost and have a few before we headed home.

The '51 Plymouth bounded along the dirt road at the Milford town dump, skirting the piles of refuse — broken baby carriages, stove pipes, brown paper bags of garbage and boxes of old clothes. When we arrived at the entry shack, Bill, a friend of my father's who ran the dump, leaned out the window. Bill was tall and skinny. When he leaned out the window of the guard shack, it seemed his body from his head to his belt was as long as an entire human being. He had a messed up mop of black hair and a thick black moustache. He smiled and asked, "What are you dumping?"

"We're not dumping," my old man said and laughed. "This is a pick up." He pointed his finger like it was a gun as we drove by. The men had thought it funny, but Pudge and I both glanced at each other and made that face that said, *Adults are weird.*

We pulled up behind the shoe-shop truck parked inside the gate and just beyond the shack. The men got out, so we did too.

"Don't go too far," Pudge's old man said.

"Hey," I said when I noticed what looked like a pile of twisted metal on the other side of the dirt road. "Can I have that bike?"

"Sure," Scrapper Jack said. "You can take anything you

want. It's a dump. Put it in the trunk."

We walked off until we were out of sight of our fathers. I sat on top of a garbage heap and had a smoke. Then I took a busted lamp made out of a candle pin, the 24-inch girl's Schwinn, and an army-surplus canteen with no cap, and I put them into the trunk of the Plymouth. When we got back into the car, all smiles and reeking of tobacco smoke and dump, I noticed there were about ten shoe boxes in the back seat. I opened one. They were pairs of shoes, brand new. I could see my father through the windshield. He stood next to the front fender, waving at the driver of the shoe-shop truck as it pulled out. As he got into the car, he turned back to me and explained. "Water damage."

"They don't look damaged," I answered, and we all laughed.

Later, at home, while working on the bike, a bit of wisdom occurred to me. The shoes my father's friend had spirited out of the shop disguised as water-damaged goods had replaced the fantasy of the church's "thou shalt not steal" with the worldly reality of "necessity is the mother of invention."

I pulled the chain guard off the bike from the dump

and attached it onto my own bike. Now I wouldn't have to roll up my pants to the knee anymore to keep the cuff from getting rolled up in the chain. I did understand, however, that I would still confess the stealing and the smoking to Father Carbary, at confession. I loved this religion where you could do whatever you needed to do to survive and then be forgiven for it that very afternoon, as long as you sinned on Saturday, the day when the priest held confessions. If you sinned on, say, a Monday, you had to be very careful that you didn't die before Saturday, since no one wanted to die in a state of sin. I tried to never sin early in the week.

My bicycle work done, I reclaimed my place on the porch chair. I was just getting comfortable when my brother Neil, the youngest in our family of seven kids, who was just about to enter the first grade, descended about halfway down the inside stairs from our apartment and said, "You have to come upstairs."

"Why?"

"I don't know. Dad wants you."

Neil was an obvious mix of Hourihan on my father's side and Williams on my mother's. Most of us were more heavily Hourihan, tall and thin. Neil was short and stocky on his French side but with Irish blue eyes, blond hair, and a serious yearning to beat someone to a pulp.

"Shit," I said to myself. I knew that bad words were a venial sin, but I wasn't sure about the status of it if I didn't say it out loud, and Sister John Gertrude had told us, if you weren't sure if something you did was a sin, it probably wasn't one.

"Does he seem mad?" I asked Neil as we walked up the stairs.

He made a face that to me meant he believed I was stupid to ask a six-year-old if he knew what my father was thinking. I opened the door to the apartment and let Neil walk in first, just in case. I was confused. There in front of me stood the whole family. Nancy and Sheila, the twins, sat at the kitchen table with my mother and father. Patty and Diane stood behind my mother. Dennis stood beside my father, who turned toward Neil and me as we entered and shut the door.

"Good," he said. "We're all here. We have to talk."

This had never happened before, but I was happy because the presence of all my brothers and sisters meant this meeting wasn't about the cigarettes at the dump.

Scrapper Jack took a tug from his coffee, and after putting down the cup, placed both hands flat on the table. "We just got a call from Dr. Allen. Dennis' asthma is getting worse." Dennis was almost apologetic, as if it was his fault for having asthma. He had been sick most of his young life and even spent a few months at St. Vincent Hospital with pneumonia.

"We have to move," my father said.

I couldn't help thinking how this wasn't such a big deal. We had moved twice before.

"We have to move to Arizona," he continued.

Dead silence descended in the kitchen. In 1956, the distance between Massachusetts and Arizona was akin to the distance between earth and the moon.

"What?" I almost shouted. I wouldn't have known I had said it out loud if everyone hadn't turned directly toward me.

"We have to move to Arizona. Not forever, but the air is dry out there, and it will be good for Dennis. He'll be able to breathe better," my father said. "And, I might be able to get a decent job."

"When?" Diane asked.

"Soon," my mother answered.

Again, there was a lull.

Patty broke the silence. "I'm not going," she said. My oldest sister, a 17-year-old senior at St. Mary's Central Catholic High School, was fiercely independent and determined to be the first in our extended family to go to college. Patricia was a beautiful blonde with blue eyes, a great figure, and a brain.

"Jesus, Mary, and Joseph. Of course you're going," my father said, and he smiled.

"No. I'm not. I have one year left in school, and I have the best grades in the class. If I stay here, I'll get a scholarship and go to college. If I go to Arizona, I won't get anything." She shrugged and said again, "I'm not going."

My Irish father seemed proudly irritated at the defiance of his oldest child. He thought for a few seconds, then looked at my mother. "We'll figure something out," he said. My mother smiled and nodded.

"Is that all?" I asked, waiting to see if anyone else — Nancy, Sheila or Diane, anyone — was going to revolt, but they all seemed okay so far with the move. Sheila and Nancy were considered very attractive, but of course they were to be forever the younger brown-haired sisters of Patty and Diane, who were known to be two of the most beautiful girls in town. Of course, they were older and had tits.

"No," my father continued. "There's something else. We can't all go together. We don't have enough money."

Splitting the family was not something that could even be thought of, but here my father was telling us it would happen. It was as if he had suggested the inevitability of each of us suffering multiple amputations.

"Who's going first?" Diane asked after several silent seconds.

"We thought you, Dennis, Johnny, and me," my father answered. "Then later, when we can get enough money, Mum, Neil, Patty and the twins will join us." His attention settled on his oldest daughter. "But maybe we can find something else for Patty." In the end, she stayed with my Aunt Adele and Uncle Jimmy to finish high school.

The part of my heart that had frozen with the loss of our home grew colder with the understanding that I would be going first. I thought of the only town I knew of in Arizona, one that I had seen on TV. "Will we be living in the Tombstone Territory?" I asked.

"No, Phoenix," my mother, Sweet Genevieve, answered.

"Will we live on a ranch?" I asked. My father had always wanted to be a cowboy, and westerns were his favorite stories, so mine were too. I fully expected to see Indians and cowboys in my new home and live on a ranch with horses and a bunk house.

My father looked at my mother and shrugged.

"I don't know," she said. "Maybe."

"Will there be Indians?"

"Probably."

That night, in bed but before sleep, I was reminded of a half-painted plank that rose up the side of the stairway at Bickford Shoe where I used to wait for Dad so we could walk home.

One day, I didn't see him coming until he was sitting right beside me.

"This is a good idea," he said, hunkering down. "The stairway keeps the wind off you." He admired my ability to keep warm in a Salvation Army cloth jacket.

It was a comfortably brisk fall day, so we decided to sit awhile, and whenever we sat awhile, he told stories. After all, he was true Irish. Tall, black hair, blue eyes. "Not a bit o' Viking blood in me," he said to me one afternoon pulling nails out of boards in the barn.

This day I remember, he told of a train ride he took in the 1930s across the dust bowl and into California hoping for work in the fields. He also told of the conductor who threw cans of peaches off the back of the train as it rumbled through the tent cities lulling the hobos to sleep through the fear of the smell of kerosene. "And Jocko," he said wide-eyed, "the adults scrambled for the cans like kiddos, with no reservations and only what pride the times had left them. They groveled in the cinders and the dirt beside the tracks to get a fair share of food."

He took out his Luckies, tapped one on a thumbnail to

tighten the tobacco, and then offered me one by holding the pack in front of me. I laughed. He did too because he thought it was a joke — thought I didn't smoke because I was only nine years old.

I rolled over in bed and remembered how he went on to tell of Woody Guthrie, his favorite musician.

"Woody would stop in the camps or in the factories and sing his songs until they threw him out. He'd be singing 'Birmingham Jail' and 'This Land is Your Land' and songs about hobos and drifters and unions. He told of workers, just like us, who were killed in a plane crash in a place called Los Gatos, and no one even cared who they were, Jocko. Woody told of beatings and the unbeatable spirit of just plain folk who had hard lives just like us."

The trip did not end as he thought it would. Scrapper Jack had been lied to, and there was no job where he had been sent. "But I met a guy in a bar," he says, "who said Contadina was hiring, so we hopped a train and rode on to the fields. The guy who did the hiring was from Milford, and he gave me a job. Turned out it paid less than he said, but I got to send some home to your mother and Patty." The rest of the family, at the time, hadn't arrived yet.

These stories must be why I grew up praying to be a hobo at Halloween. They were my heroes. The hardened men, women, and children who worked the fields and for whom there was no free lunch, even when it was "free."

He was out there long enough for his clothes to change colors where he sweated the most, and then jobs opened up in the shoe shops back in Massachusetts, so he came home. He brought with him the stories of the last depression, of Woody and the road, and he sang his songs to us every night. I rode along with him and Guthrie and absorbed a unique understanding of the ways of the world. An understanding I hoped would never come in handy.

As he flipped away his cigarette in the practiced way a working man does, he said, "Jocko, if you got your principles intact, I've always said, 'Deal me your hardest card. I'll win this gorram game.'"

The remembrance of his trip across the country helped me sleep in the face of my own upcoming trip.

Chapter Three
Moving West
September

In early September, but before school started for the year, I found myself sitting in the back of Jimmy's Taxi with my brother Dennis. The cab parked outside our Pine Street apartment provided confirmation enough that we were, in fact, moving to Arizona.

My younger brother and I had suitcases piled between us on the seat and others stacked on the floor of the cab. He looked at me, peering over the top of the suitcases. All I could see of him was his black hair, the top of his head, and his eyes. Then his fingers appeared on the top of the suitcase on either side of his head. He pulled himself up so I could see the rest of his face. He smiled and said simply, "This is stupid."

We laughed, knowing that things my family did were not usually the norm. Family life for us resembled something like, "It's going to be a rough ride. Hold on or fall off," and none of us had fallen off yet. We were just that good at hanging on. Dennis was sick. He had asthma, and we were moving across the country so he could get better. In my family, that made sense.

My father settled into the front passenger side, and we all waited for Diane. She appeared in the doorway of the house clutching her Maybelline makeup case. Fifteen years old, but appearing like she was twenty, she stopped for a few seconds for effect, and then she came down the stairs to the sidewalk where the rest of my family stood ready to say goodbye. She shook back her long black hair and hugged Neil and the twins. Then she hugged my mother. When she stopped, I noticed my mother's eyes were watering. Diane climbed into the cab and said, "Bye Neil. Bye Nancy, Sheila, Mum. Bye Patty's clothes," and my brother, my father, myself, and my new fifteen-year-old mother/sister were whisked up Pine Street and eventually out Route 16 toward the Framingham train station thirty miles away.

In Framingham, we unloaded. We dragged and carried our suitcases to the back of the station, track side, and piled them against the wall of the building. Since Diane had three of the biggest suitcases, I guessed she hadn't said goodbye to all of Patty's clothes. I sat on one of the bigger suitcases, and my sight settled on the four sets of tracks in front of me. Across them, and then across a small vacant lot, was a multi-story white building with a sign on top that said HOTEL. I wondered how many people might be coming into the station from all over the country and staying in that hotel. It made me wonder for the first time where we would be living, now that we had no home. For the first time, I fully realized I would be leaving my mother and the loving protection of St. Mary's, I wondered if Jesus knew where we were going, but before I could think about it any further, my father showed up from inside the building. He held tickets in one hand and a paper cup of hot coffee in the other.

"It will be about an hour's wait," he said. "Get comfortable."

We were to take the train to Chicago and then a bus to the Wild West. The methods of transportation had laid to rest the thought that we might be outrunning the Indians, who I figured would most likely want to attack the train as they always did in the movies. To me, the West was only what I had seen on TV or heard about in my father's bedtime stories. The advancements that had been made between the 1850s and the 1950s had yet to be made clear to Hollywood, or to me.

It was warm for a New England September. I leaned back against the granite wall that reminded me of the school that had, for five years, been my home away from home. I hadn't said goodbye to any of my friends except Pudge. I didn't know I was supposed to. I didn't know if I would miss them, or if they would miss me. This move across the known world was new to me. The other end of this trip was, in my mind, just a black hole with maybe some Indians.

I must have dozed off and dreamed about being dragged by a crazy nun up Winter Street and into the church. In the dream, a priest prayed over me, and his accent turned his monotone mumblings, salted with the names of various saints, into a babble the consistency of pudding. I could see the statues of Joseph and Mary staring down at me from the altar, and I wanted to know if they understood what was happening and whose side they were on. I awakened abruptly in a cold sweat.

A train screeched across Main Street and down the track only twenty feet from where I sat. The hiss of the locomotive belching steam from under the wheels, the metallic scream of the brakes, and the smell of what could only be that of fire and brimstone was exciting. It was the opening chapter of my new life.

"Is this it?" I asked my father. "Is this our train?"

"That's it, Jocko," he said, and he woke Dennis, who had fallen asleep in a wooden chair against the wall. I looked at my younger brother and realized for the first time that he favored my father more than I did. My father moved the luggage closer to the train, and, when it stopped completely, some men came and started loading them. Diane appeared down the walkway beside the track. I had no idea where she had been, but I followed her and Dennis up the metal steps and onto the train. As I was about to step onto the landing between the cars, my father hooked a finger into my belt and pulled me back a bit.

"Hold on," he said, and pointed up to the front of the iron horse, past it, and up along the tracks that led to New York.

"By the time you're my age, this will all be gone."

"What?" I asked.

"All of it; the tracks, the station, the trains, the steam, all of it will be gone."

I had no idea what he was talking about, but it seemed important to him, so I nodded solemnly like I always did with the nuns at school. Then I stepped onto the platform between the two cars, took a right, and pushed inside the doors of the passenger car. We would ride this to New York, switch trains, and lumber on to Chicago. I slept most of the way, waking up only when the conductor would shout "Passengers will please refrain," each time the train stopped to let people on or off.

Before we had traveled ten minutes, I saw a second track. It ran alongside us, and I imagined I rode on a train all my own, riding along the other track. I hadn't left the seat on the train, but I was simultaneously on the imagined train. The biggest difference between the two trains was that on the one I sat in I was being swept along wherever the train took me, and on the other track I was in control and trying to keep up. When it periodically disappeared, I found ways to imagine myself jumping from tree to tree or careening along rooftops. No matter what appeared or disappeared, I found a way to continue on. When there were lakes, I skimmed. When there were forests, I skipped along tree tops. When we chugged alongside roadways, I sat on top of the cars and waved back at myself leaning against the train window. As we raced behind the backs of buildings in cities, my other self climbed along the building tops. My second-train fantasy kept me from facing the fact that I was headed into a place totally foreign to me, forced to leave everything I knew behind.

In Chicago, we boarded a Greyhound bus and headed south, and without the twin train track, my avatar disappeared. I travelled on alone, without my mother, without half of my family, without my friends, without my religion. My eyes were about to be opened. I was to face the reality that my life, as it had been, was over, and something new was about to happen. I guess I wasn't sure which of me would arrive in Phoenix, the one being swept along or the one in control? I wondered if I would ever be welcomed home again.

After several hours of small towns going backwards, one after another, in the bus window, we stopped at a station somewhere in the South. The numbing rumble of Eisenhower's highways had drugged me to the point where I had reached an altered state of irresponsible existence. There was no school, which was a good thing, but there was no baseball, which wasn't so good. Somewhere in the murky middle of my trip, I was sleep deprived, and I stunk. We stopped to change buses.

It was an oppressive afternoon as I stepped from the bus into the dark garage where all the buses parked while passengers went inside to be fed, watered, and relieved. I had trouble breathing. I could exhale fine, but my body revolted against breathing the heated air into my lungs, as if I couldn't accept anything more. The diesel smell of the bus exhaust made me light-headed as we walked through the garage and to the station door. The black asphalt rippled in the heat haze as my father held the door open for us. We went by him into the yellow indoor light and the drowsed crowd of passengers waiting on rows of wooden benches, reading newspapers, sleeping with their mouths opened, or fanning themselves slowly with hats. Large metal propeller-like fans at each end of the room were losing the battle against the suffocating heat of the afternoon. I headed for the water fountain, with my father close behind.

Scrapper Jack was a boxer, a shoe worker, and an Irishman; not in that order. Our common ground was baseball. We loved the Red Sox now that the Braves had left town, but, of course, we loved The Mick too and Jackie Robinson.

A line of people snaked from the water fountain, and a group of three or four people at the end groused about the fat guy who seemed to be trying to drink all the water that was left in the pipes. Someone called him a camel, and Scrapper Jack laughed.

I turned back across the room to see my brother and sister had found an open bench and were sitting and staring into the heat.

I stepped out of line and peered along the queue of sweaty shirts and hiked up skirts.

Then I learned something I hadn't known before. There was a second fountain. A perfectly empty fountain, sitting alone, exactly like the one we were headed to, except it didn't have a line. I couldn't believe these people were all so locked in place that they couldn't see it. I shot a glance back at my father. He had seen it too. He looked at it and turned back to me. He seemed sad.

"How come?" I asked him.

"Read the sign," he said.

Over the line I stood in, tacked on the wall, a stark sign read "WHITE."

Over the other it said "COLORED."

It made no sense to me. We were all people in various stages of dehydration. Thirst and hunger were common to all of us. If left without water, in this heat, I supposed we would all die. We were all sweltering hot, and we all needed water. But first, we felt we had to be separated by the color of our skin before we quenched our thirst. It was what Dennis would have called "just stupid."

The only "colored" man I had ever met was Buster, who brought the take-home hats to my mother in the white panel truck. My mother would always make sure there was soda for Buster on the hot days, which I liked because he always shared it with me.

I focused again on Scrapper Jack. He was assessing the other people in the line now, anticipating my question.

"Can I drink out of that one?" I asked. A few people who had huddled into line behind us laughed. He wasn't moving, but he had put his hand on the back of my neck like he always did when we walked down the street.

"Well," he counseled, "Jackie Robinson, if he was here, would drink out of that one."

He scrutinized me while he kept his eye on the crowd of people. The fat camel guy walked by, wiping his mouth. He stopped for a quick look at me when Scrapper Jack said, "Just keep moving," and he did.

I knew what he meant. He always told me to play like Robinson. He called him "fearless." He said Robinson had "intestinal fortitude." So he said this thing about Robinson, and then he squatted down to eye-level as if he had made a decision.

"And he wouldn't be allowed to drink out of this one."

I thought back to sharing an icy cold Miscoe Springs orange soda with my parents' friend Buster on the bumper of his hat-shop truck. He was my friend too, and he wouldn't be allowed to drink here either.

"What's the difference?" I asked.

He stepped out of line and scrutinized more of the

people who were all facing us now for some strange reason, and he said, "It's your call."

We always spoke baseball in those days. I guess when you don't have a lot going for you, you're drawn to the fairness of the game.

"I guess I'm not thirsty," I said, because I could tell drinking in one line was going to cause some serious problems, and I sure wasn't going to drink somewhere that Jackie Robinson and Buster weren't allowed. Because I realized, even then, that I had more in common with them than with the people in that line at the WHITE water fountain. I decided not to drink at all.

This was the day I found that bigotry, the opium of the ignorant, isn't inborn.

It occurred to me later in life that Scrapper Jack was ready to take on anyone in that crowded southern bus terminal rather than let his kid grow up a racist. As we started to leave, I glanced hopefully at the men's room door.

"Same thing there?" I asked.

"Yup," he said. "Get on the bus. I have to buy some cigarettes."

But I had to go. It took me a few minutes of deciding, and I guess he had bought his smokes and climbed back on the bus by the time I arrived in the garage. I decided to pee against the wall of the station in full view of the people already on the bus. I figured anyone could pee there no matter what color your skin was. I knew there was a toilet on the bus, but I had a point to make. It was a statement between me and God. When I finally got on the bus, a bunch of people stood up and applauded. As I sat down Scrapper Jack leaned over and said, "I told them why you did that, peed against the building. I think they liked it." He handed me a bottle of orangeade that he must have bought while getting his cigarettes. I turned to the seat behind me where Diane and Dennis were sitting. I offered them some of the soda. Dennis took it, but I think Diane was trying to ignore the fact that she was in any way connected to this kid who would pee in public.

The trip became mind-numbing through Missouri, Oklahoma, Texas, and New Mexico. I thought it out, and I settled on the fact that I had broken the human law about not peeing against the wall in public because to pee where I was told to pee would break the laws I had been taught in school and at home all my life.

Finally, the bus pulled onto the city streets of Phoenix. I watched the people on the sidewalk, and suddenly one man caught my eye. He wore a cowboy hat, cowboy boots, and a pair of six guns in holsters on his hips. I nudged my father and pointed at the man.

"Damn," my father said. "We're not in Massachusetts anymore."

Chapter Four
Knowledge and Understanding
September

I had been introduced religiously by Baptism as a baby to what were to be the rules of life, and in the second grade I had trudged up the aisle of the church with my classmates to receive our first Holy Communion. I guess this trip to Arizona was to be my journey toward the next big sacrament: Confirmation.

We stood at the lunch counter of the Phoenix Greyhound station not knowing where we would be going next. "Get them an orangeade," my father said to Diane and pointed to a booth. To my father, all drinks that had no alcohol in them were "orangeade." While we sat and waited, he talked with the manager who kept peeking over my father's shoulder at Diane. Dad came to the table after a few minutes and said, "We can get a room upstairs. Let's go."

Let's go? Are you kidding me? Dennis and I each had a full glass of Coca Cola. It wasn't a store brand. It was the real thing. We didn't even have to share it. We weren't going anywhere until those glasses were empty. So we stood there chugging the Coke while my father and sister waited. It turned into a race, and the soda dribbled down my chin and onto my shirt. We finished together and laughed.

We stepped outside into the hot, exhaust-filled smell. The street gutters were full with rainwater. This year, the rainy season had ended early, but I had never seen it rain, and wouldn't until the next summer. We only had to take a few steps before we came to the door that said "ROOMS." It opened to a dark stairway. We stepped inside and were engulfed by the heavy smell of a late summer dead zone. It smelled like a men's room. We climbed the dark wooden stairs to the second floor, and my old man opened the door to the room at the top. As hot as the air in the hallway was, what escaped the room in a gust was even more stifling. I didn't know it, but I was about to acquire knowledge that would become part of my being for the rest of my life.

I peeked around my father's leg into our room, and I winced.

A single round light clutched the center of a smoke-stained ceiling in the dark space. My father flipped the switch a few times to make sure it worked and then left it off. Across the room a pair of dark brown painted-shut windows, half-shaded but curtainless, looked down like tired eyes onto the baked and bustling street. We pushed the suitcases inside, and I flopped on the bed, exhausted from four days and three nights of traveling, half of it in a Scenicruiser with an erratic air conditioner. I stunk and my hair hurt.

I rolled onto my side on the center of the bed, moved to the edge so Dennis could fit, and I inspected the room. Beside me, dust floated in the sunlight from the two windows. They were huge and took up most of the wall except that they were separated by a useless hot water radiator. All I could see outside were the tops of the buildings across the street and a perfectly empty blue sky.

On the end wall was a squat, dark brown dresser with a dirty mirror, next to it was a sink with two faucets, one hot, one warm, and next to that was a black wastebasket with a cattle-drive scene painted in the center of a circular lariat.

The door stood in the far end of the next wall, and

beside it sat a roll-top desk with a green-shaded desk lamp. Next to me was the second bed. Beneath the pilled and yellowed bed spreads were blue and white thin-striped pillows with no cases.

My father left us sprawled on the beds. "I'll be back," he said and locked the door softly.

We had no trouble sleeping, despite the fact that we were enveloped by a crushing, dry, oven-like heat. When he returned, he told Diane to put on some clean clothes. They left again, and when they returned, even though she was too young to work legally, she had a job as a waitress at the Greyhound station luncheonette, and he had an interview as produce manager at a Bayless market. I figured they had lied about Diane's age. "Thou shalt not lie," kept creeping into my mind, but for years I had been pulled further and further away from my religious upbringing by the necessities of our life: reality over fantasy.

They also had bags of food, which they emptied into the middle drawer of the bureau. There was mustard and bologna and bread, some apples and nectarines, aspirin for my nagging toothache that had begun somewhere near Albuquerque, New Mexico, and four Cracker Jack boxes.

That night, I woke around ten. The pain was digging

up through one of my back teeth into the roof of my mouth. It was the worst toothache I had ever had. The only thing that calmed the drilling pain was to swish the warm metallic water from the tap around in my mouth, and it only worked for about fifteen minutes each time.

"Jocko," my father announced. "We can't see a dentist until tomorrow morning. You're just going to have to tough it out."

Trying to keep my mind off the pain, he told stories of taking the train in the 30s out to California to work the Contadina tomato fields and send money home, and he told tall tales about the hobos he met along the way.

He sang The Big Rock Candy Mountain over and over again and recalled the history of Woody Guthrie until finally around three a.m. I told him, "Dad, go to bed. I can take care of this myself. You gotta get a job tomorrow. We're running out of baloney, and the fruit is gonna go bad."

He laughed, laid back in the bed, and went to sleep.

He had come here with half his family, with no wife, no place to stay, little money, and no job. It must have taken courage. And now he was going to put off his job interview to get me to the dentist in the morning. The least I could do was take care of my own tooth that night.

All night I prayed to God in the hopes He could do

something about the pain in my jaw from this damn tooth. I could see no reason why He wouldn't want to help me, but like the nuns always said, sometimes God says, "No." It continued to hurt. The pain even seemed to get worse, and I wondered why, after all I had been through in the name of God, He wouldn't help me. It seemed that each year we had become more and more separated, and it wasn't my doing. But in the morning Diane woke up while my father slept. She dressed and came over to where I sat. I had pulled the only chair up to the window and was staring out past the buildings to the south where I could see the mountains. Diane scribbled a note on some paper that had been left on the small desk, put it on the pillow next to my father, fished some money out of his wallet, and nudged me to follow her into the hallway.

"I found out where the dentist is," she said as she quietly closed the door to the room behind us. "I told Dad to go ahead and get his job. We can do this, right?"

"Sure," I said. The only thing I wanted was for the pain to stop. I would have walked with the devil into hell if I had the promise of the pain being gone.

"It's not far," she said. She lied. We seemingly walked forever, and then in a single story sprawling building, surrounded by ornamental orange trees that tasted more like lemons than oranges, we found the dentist's office.

I sat in the empty waiting room and stared at the clock on the wall. It read 7:43.

"He'll be in at eight," Diane said. My barely teenage sister stepped up to the window where the woman was putting away her pocketbook and setting her coffee on the desk. Diane stood and negotiated how much money it would cost to get my tooth pulled.

"I can't pay that," she said to the woman's first offer. I thought, "Oh, for God's sake, pay it." There was more mumbling. Diane nodded at the next offer and paid, and then she returned to sit beside me.

"How is it?" she asked.

I thought of several bad words, but settled on, "It hurts."

It seemed like hours before I was sitting in the chair with the little porcelain sink beside me. The dentist in his white coat entered and stood beside me, holding a syringe.

"It will be a little pinch," he said and looked into my mouth from only a foot from my face. I could smell his breakfast, and it made me feel sick. He stuck the syringe into my mouth.

"Shit," I said out loud. It felt as if he had shoved that needle all the way into my brain. I was getting more than a little fed up with people lying to me that morning.

"Okay, it will be numb in few minutes," he said, and he left the room.

I hoped the shot would numb it a bit further, but he re-entered only minutes later and said, "Is it numb yet?"

"No," I said truthfully. The tooth still hurt.

"Sure it is," he said and sidled up to my left side with some kind of pliers in his hand.

"It's not numb yet," I said again, louder.

He stopped for a second and grimaced down at me. He had a big nose. "Look," he said. "I know what I'm doing. I gave you a shot of Novocain that made it numb. It works fast, so your tooth is numb."

I felt it. I knew if he started pulling that thing out of there it was going to hurt like hell. He leaned over and began to stick the pliers into my mouth. I panicked. Almost before I even knew I had thrown a punch, I saw his nose bleeding all over his white dentist's coat.

My mother had told me that no one had a right to put their hands on me if I said no, and my father had taught me it only took about seven pounds of pressure to break a nose. I guess he was right. The dentist's nose was definitely broken.

He headed for the waiting room, striding without acknowledging me. I followed him, pulling off the paper bib and saying, "I told you it isn't numb."

He had grabbed a Kleenex and held it to his nose, but it wasn't helping.

As soon as he saw Diane, he shouted, "Get nis animaaw out o heah."

"What?" she said. I guess it wasn't a great idea for her to be laughing, but the others in the waiting room were laughing too. He took the wad of Kleenex away from his nose and said again, "Get this animal out of here!"

Then came the words I would remember forever as my beautiful black-haired sister stood up, took my hand, and in front of the now-crowded room said, "Awww, did the little boy hurt the big dentist? He told you it wasn't numb. We all heard him."

"Get out!"

She didn't even turn around. As we walked through the doors, she sang back to him, "You should have listened."

Everyone laughed again, and she led me proudly out of the office into the street.

"Sorry," I said.

"Listen to me," she said, stopping and turning toward me. "There are plenty of things you're going to do wrong. You can be sorry for them, but don't be sorry for stuff that isn't your fault." It was a bit of knowledge I would take with me for the rest of my life.

On the walk home, I realized the Novocain had begun working, so as we walked down the sidewalk, I pulled my own tooth. I couldn't let my father pay for something and then not have it happen. We didn't have that kind of money. I showed it to Diane, and she laughed.

Dad was home by late morning, and Diane went to her new job downstairs. She took Dennis down to sit at a corner table in the luncheonette, and Dad took me with him out onto the sidewalk in front of the station. The water in the gutters had all evaporated in the incessant heat. We seemed to walk forever, down the wide sidewalks lined by thirty-foot palm trees.

He was having a hard time looking at me while he explained how I shouldn't punch a dentist in the face. He almost seemed to be fighting off laughter. He did say he understood that I had a pretty good reason to "pop the fool." But that I shouldn't do it again. He finally turned to face me and added, "Unless, of course, the situation calls for it. I guess it's your call."

We stopped in front of a church. He started to go up the steps, stopped, thought, then said, "You sit over here on this wall. I'll be right out." I guess he was afraid I would punch someone else if things didn't go right.

"In all my livin' life," he said almost to himself as he

walked away toward the front door of the church, shaking his head. He turned back for a second, and smiling, he said, "You're a real corker, you are."

I wasn't sure, but I thought it was a compliment, so I said, "Thanks, Dad."

While he was gone, I watched the people passing by on the sidewalk. They were similar to the people on the Main Street in Milford, except for a few differences. For one, a lot of the men wore six-guns, in holsters, belts with huge buckles, and cowboy hats, and the women wore less clothing than I had ever seen before. Even in summer in New England, I had never seen these kinds of halter tops or short shorts, and from my height as a child the view of halter tops was enlightening. After a while, I moved to the shade under a bush. It occurred to me that something was very different here. I didn't know any of the people. I didn't know where they lived. I didn't know their families. I didn't even know what was at the end of this road in front of me. *If my father never comes out of that church, will I be able to survive?* I wondered. Would I even be able to find my way back to the bus station?

As a bus stopped and then left, I realized I should not be walking around in life with no money in my pocket. It dawned on me that my life, since I had arrived at the Greyhound station, was totally empty of knowledge except what I had carried with me onto the train in Framingham. I didn't have to worry for long. More knowledge was about to be imparted to me.

My father stormed out of the church and down the steps.

"Look at this," he said and handed me a Gulf road map of Phoenix. "I asked the priest if he could help us find a place to rent, and he gave me this. Come on," he said. He grabbed my hand and pulled me with him down the street. "Damn priest called me a Yankee," he said, sort of to himself. It made no sense to me, since we were Red Sox people.

"Where are we going?" I asked.

"I'm not sure yet," he said, but we kept walking.

It wasn't comforting that I was being led by someone who didn't know where he was going, but I figured he was my only hope.

After a very hot twenty minutes or so of me trying to keep up, he said, "Here we are."

We stood in front of a place called "The Silver Dollar Bar and Grille."

"Stay here" he said. He pointed at a bench at roadside. "I'll be right out." As I sat down, I glanced up at the sign that said "Bus Stop." There was another bench beside the one I sat on. I figured there were signs over them like the ones in the bus station, so I didn't check. This is where I sat, and this is where I would be.

I'm sure he had time for a quick beer, and then he came out smiling and waving a torn piece of yellow paper that he held between his thumb and pointing finger. It appeared to have been ripped out of the yellow pages of the phone book. Instead of walking on, he sat down next to me on the bench.

"Let that be a lesson to you, Jocko."

"What?" I really had no idea what he was talking about, but he kept waving that piece of paper.

"This is the address of our new place." He looked again at the paper. "South Second Street. Let that be a lesson to you," he repeated. "If you need help, never ask a priest. If you need help, ask a bartender."

I nodded at him with feigned understanding.

"We got a place," he said. "We can move there tomorrow."

"How about the job?" I asked.

"Oh, right. I made a call. I got that too. I'm the produce manager at Bayless in South Phoenix. It's walking distance from our place. Let's go." We started our trek back uptown as the sun beat down on us. Breathing in the Arizona desert was like sticking your head into a pre-heated oven and inhaling. I guess it felt good to Dennis, though. It had been a great day. My father had a job, my sister had a job, we wouldn't have to live at the bus station any longer, we had our own place, my toothache was gone, and Dennis could breathe. I also counted it as a good thing that it was heading into mid-September, and my father hadn't mentioned school yet.

The next morning, we all went down to the luncheonette and had breakfast. I had a vanilla frappe. Of course, here I had to call it a milk shake. The other waitress told me that "frappe" was "what we all call pigeon crap." I wondered if that was where we too got the name for a vanilla frappe. The consistency was pretty similar. I guess the toothache and the bus ride and the train ride had taken its toll on my body. I finished my vanilla pigeon-crap breakfast, threw up under the table, cleaned it up, and we piled into a cab to see our new place. Diane gave me some gum.

South Second Street was a dirt road. At the end of it, an irrigation ditch ran right across in front of us. The taxi took a right and stopped.

My new home loomed in front of us. A shiver ran up my spine.

"Damn," I said.

A few feet off the dirt driveway was a long building

that Scrapper Jack called a "Quonset hut." It was one story and had in it five different apartments. On the rear side of the building was a fenced-off auto junk yard. The ditch in the front ran along on the other side of the driveway, and after that a piece of the desert baked in the sun. Across the desert, I could see the range that I found out later was called the Superstition Mountains.

Our place was to be the second apartment from the left. We each dragged a suitcase from the back seat or the trunk of the taxi and huddled at the front door as my father fished out the key.

An attractive but very thin woman from next door stood with her two boys, watching us as we started to enter the place.

"You might want to check for snakes and scorpions before you take your stuff in," she counseled. "Nobody's been there for a while."

Our new life had begun.

The apartment wasn't even as big as our Purchase Street home. Just inside the door there was the ten-by-ten living room and a tiny kitchen with the back door. There were two smaller bedrooms. Dennis and I set up in one, and my father in the other, and Diane on the couch in the living room. The kitchen had a real large tin sink, which was good since it had to be used to wash both our dishes and our clothes. The clothes lines in the backyard were strung from the house to the fence that separated our yard from the junkyard.

Just as we finished settling in, the boys from next door came to introduce themselves.

One was my size. The other was a head and shoulders bigger than me and twice as wide. It turned out the one who was my size, Garrett, was a few years younger than me, and the giant, Posey, was only one year younger than me.

Garrett had a nearly shaved head. He was thin and wiry, and if Olive Oyl was a boy, she would have looked like Garrett. Posey was huge for his age. He had a big round head, beady eyes, and a natural snarl. Posey made the introduction.

"Hi, I'm Posey. He's Garrett. My mum said we should come on over and find out if y'all needed some help gettin' stuff done."

Diane thanked them and asked where some things were, like the nearest drug store and public swimming pool. They drew her a map, and then they went home.

That afternoon, we met their father.

He stood just inside our front door. "Everyone calls me Duke," said the big man. Duke was at least as much bigger than my father as Posey was bigger than me.

"Ah hear y'all are from Boston. So…" He stuck his huge hand out to my father to shake, "Ah guess ah'll be callin' you Mr. Boston." He turned to me. "An you'll be l'il Boston." Now it was Dennis' turn. "And who are you?"

My younger brother stared up at our new acquaintance, unafraid of his size. "I guess you'll be calling me Dennis Hourihan," he said. He turned and walked back into our bedroom. It didn't occur to me at the time, but Dennis was old for his age.

We had only found one scorpion and no snakes. The venomous bug scuttled under the living room couch. Posey had picked it up on a piece of cardboard, taken it outside, and stepped on it, crushing it dead against the hard-packed desert dirt that was our front yard We all slept just fine that night, and it wasn't long before we were used to our new surroundings.

It was curious that the Texan children and the Tennessee kids, who lived on the other side of our place, and even the two girls in the next place, were gone all day, so I asked Posey about it one late afternoon. He told me they had to go to school. I didn't bring it up with my father. I figured he had enough on his mind. Instead, Dennis and I spent our time outside catching frogs and crayfish and cooling off in the irrigation ditch whenever it was flooded.

Within a few weeks, a new family from Missouri moved into one of the other apartments. The eleven-year-old boy in the family was red-haired Crazy Willie.

Posey, Garrett, Willie, and the redneck brothers, Tim and Danny Boy, became my friends. We spent most of September shooting marbles, flying kites, and throwing hunting knives at each other. Of course, we also made sling shots and fired them over the deserted building just off our yard and onto the main road where the market and the Silver Dollar Bar and Grille were. When we were done for the day, we would walk over and see how many windows had been broken.

Early in October, Posey suggested, "Let's go on down to Safeway and watch Ned the Butcher cut up a cow."

We spent the next handful of Sundays going down religiously to the butcher's shed to watch Ned's ritual of making hamburger from scratch. It was sort of like going to church, only Jesus was a cow.

This first day we walked across a half-mile of desert, down below our neighborhood that Posey and Garrett's mother Dodee called "our barrio," jumped the irrigation ditch, cut through the orange grove, and slipped down the powder-dirt road to the tin-roofed wooden building with the holding pen outside. In the holding pen was a cow that had, for today, been the chosen one. There was a big rock under a chestnut tree where we sat and ate pomegranates from the tree behind us, about ten yards from the birth of hamburger. It was there that I found the understanding that my favorite sustenance began as a live being. Ned would walk the cow to the holding pen that was built a lot like one of those bull-riding chutes at the rodeo. He would drop a heavy chain over her back and have her carry it into the pen. They'd both look at us. It always seemed that the cow was trying to tell us something that we just weren't understanding. It was sort of like she was being sacrificed for the greater good of mankind. The greater good being hamburgers and meatloaf. Ned would nod and then begin.

First, he attached the chain to the winch above the pen. He pulled it up and hung it over a pulley above his head, then down again to the floor, where he laid the chain out in a circle about where the cow would be standing. Ned looped it around the cow's hind leg and tightened it a bit. He then picked up his .22 rifle and walked around to the front of the pen. At this point, he'd be facing away from and directly at the cow.

He would matter-of-factly put the gun to his shoulder and lean forward to put the business end of the barrel lightly against the cow's head, right between the eyes.

The two, the cow and the man, would stare into each

other's eyes from a few feet away in total misunderstanding.

The man not realizing the cow had something very different in mind. The cow thinking whatever it was that cows think. Then Ned would pull the trigger. The cow would hit the deck. Whatever her thoughts had been just before her death, they were gone now, as the winch squealed and the chain tightened around her leg and lifted her upside down off the ground. I always wondered if she had even known she was about to die.

Sometimes, Ned would make what he called "kosher" hamburger. He would take out a big silver knife, raise it up over his head, because that was the rule, and bring it down slowly on the cow's head. Then he'd shoot her. Nobody would know the difference. According to Ned, Jewish law was preserved, and the Jewish people would be able to eat the same stuff as Christians and heathens and believe it was something different.

Ned would empty out the cow and deftly strip the hide off her.

Then he'd lop off her head.

After this point, it was a lot easier to watch because she was no longer watching back. Watching the dead cow was much easier than watching her become dead.

Ned would then split the cow in half with a cleaver. He'd cut off the hooves, throw the two sides up on a bench and hack them up into manageable pieces.

Sometimes he'd toss us the tail or the ears or the hooves. I think he expected us to make soup out of them. We just thought they were something to keep in a box in the closet.

Then he would cut up the shoulder part, cut out the bone, and toss the meat into the grinder attached to the table behind him. The meat would be taken inside the tin-roofed shed and brought into the Safeway market to be packaged in cellophane and sold to people who had no idea that, inside that neat little package, they were buying the death and mutilation of an animal.

People would walk in the front door of the supermarket as if they were stepping inside a church, no blood on their hands, no blood on their clothes, no smell of the butchering, just the manageable sustenance of a burger or a stuffed pepper. They would push a cart to the appropriate aisle, pick out a nicely wrapped pound or two of hamburger and go home for a weekend cook-out. It seemed to me that people should have to see how meat was made before they got to eat it and think they understood hamburger.

Before I left the rock every Sunday, I wondered if the cow understood that people never knew what she went through by dying so they could live. It also crossed my mind that we should be going to church on Sunday and to school on weekdays.

One Monday in October, around my birthday and only days before the rest of my family was scheduled to arrive, I had walked up to the Bayless market to meet Dad for the walk home. I liked to walk him home because to get from Bayless to our place, he had to walk past the Silver Dollar Bar and Grille. If I was with him, he couldn't go into the bar. I did this mostly because of a story Posey told me that his father had told him.

We sat in the front seat of Duke's pickup truck, parked at the end of the apartments next to Posey's place. We had collected several rocks each and were facing the auto junk yard. Every once in a while the pit bull would find his way to the fence in front of us, and we would reach out the windows and throw rocks at him. Posey got the driver's seat because he was left handed.

"My daddy says Mr. Boston was at the Silver Dollar last week, and this big drunk guy stumbled into him, and the big guy spilled a beer. He turned to Mr. Boston and said, 'You did that on purpose.' So your daddy tells him to go ef himself. And the guy turns back for a fight."

"He probably heard my father talk, right?" I asked.

"Sure enough. Y'all talk real funny. So, Mr. Boston

says to the guy, 'You see that pair of Bowie knives up there on the wall behind the bar? Why don't we each take one of those, tie our wrists together, and then whoever is still alive in a few minutes gets to be the winner?' The guy says no and slinks off to a booth in the corner. My daddy says Mr. Boston is one bad ass son a bitch."

A chill ran down my neck and down both arms, and I shuddered. All I could think of was, *"What if the guy had said yes, and Dad lost, and the three of us kids were left at home without a father? What if we had to go live in an orphanage? My mother would be really pissed when she got here."*

From that point on, whenever I could, I walked up to the supermarket where he worked and walked my father home. I figured it could keep him out of the bar, and we'd be okay until my mother got here.

This was one of those days.

My feet were dog tired from waiting for so long in the produce aisle for my father to finish work in the back room. I had just escaped an error-filled baseball practice and scuffled the half-mile or so to the store with my pudgy three-finger mitt looped through my belt, my ego bruised, and my self-esteem as a ballplayer shredded. I took five discarded Dr. Pepper bottles from the aisles where thirsty shoppers had left them, and I was carrying them through the fruit tables to the deposit register to get my dime for candy when it happened.

There in the apples was one of those out-of-place things. It was the right color — red, but it wasn't an apple.

In 1955, eight-hundred dollars was a lot of money, and as I counted the bills in the wallet that had been camouflaged among the Macs, I realized 856 dollars and a quarter, two dimes, and three pennies was even more.

I searched, but there was no one even close to me. The apple area was conveniently vacant.

I wasn't thinking of what it could buy. I wasn't thinking that, closing in on my birthday, I could have bought sneakers without holes and could get rid of the cardboard picture of Buster Brown and Tige that was protecting the bottom of my right foot from the hot sidewalk.

Scrapper Jack had been banished to stocking this produce section, an out-of-his-element, shoe factory piece-worker stacking grapefruit and nectarines for about fifty bucks a week.

I took a quick peek inside the swinging doors at the back of the store and saw that he was finishing tossing the empty tangerine crates out onto the landing — too busy for advice right now.

I counted the money again and shrugged, then returned to the apple section. The apples reminded me of original sin, so I moved on to the front of the store and the courtesy booth.

When my father got there I was turning it in, because it was the right thing to do.

"What you got there?" he asked, hooking the loop on his pricer onto his belt.

"Eight-hundred bucks or so," I said just as matter-of-factly as he had asked.

I liked to imitate him.

He stopped fumbling at his belt and leaned in to see the overstuffed wallet being passed to the woman behind the counter. The girl looked over the top of my head without moving. After a few silent minutes, she reluctantly reached across and took the wallet.

"Wait a minute," he said and reached for the wallet. She smiled and handed it to him as if that was exactly what should happen.

He fingered through the papers and found one he seemed to be expecting.

"Got a pencil?" he asked her.

He wrote something down on a piece of a register tape and stuck it in his pocket. "Make sure this gets where it's supposed to go," he said as he pushed the wallet back to her.

As we turned to walk off, the woman said, "Jack, are

you sure?"

I didn't know what the heck she meant.

It was dark when we turned onto the silted dirt of South Second Street and the line of apartments where we lived.

At the door, he gave me a little tap on the back of my head like he always did. It seemed a little stronger than usual.

I guess something was going on there, but he said, "You did the right thing, Jocko."

Middle of the next week, the store called. I had been left a reward for turning in the money. The woman hadn't even known she had lost it. She was that rich. She left me eleven dollars. "A dollar for each year of his wonderful life," she had told my father.

I bought a new glove. It had five fingers and a good pocket. It did nothing to keep me from playing ground balls off my face, but I had done what a good kid was supposed to do, what I had been taught so far in life. When you have learned about the hardships of the life of Jesus, you tend to find it easier to do things right. When you have seen how hamburger is made, you seem to appreciate your food more.

A few days later, the rest of my family arrived.

Chapter Five
Cotton Picking
October – November

I spent weeks wondering if I should have kept the wallet, but it didn't matter because I soon found other ways to get money.

My father and three of us kids had been in the desert about a month when my mother and my other siblings joined us. The market had given my father an advance on his salary to pay for the trip. Among other things, my mother bought us new underwear and made us go to school. Having no "good underwear" had been my father's excuse for not sending us to school yet, but I think it was because he didn't know how we would do in a public school where most kids spoke Spanish in the playground, and everyone laughed at the accent that I never knew I had. I think he underestimated me.

So on weekdays, we kids sweated the walk to Rio Vista school together, a half-mile trudge from the intersection of two irrigation ditches at South Second Street., along hard-packed dirt roads lined with orange, grapefruit, and pomegranate trees, and through the bull-protected barren pasture, across the lines of traffic on the boulevard — together.

We were the ones the rich people living up by Camelback Mountain called by pet names, living in rows of squalid and stifling Quonset huts along the edge of the desert like a continuous straight-line border of metal-roofed armadillos or flat-roofed squat huts with three or four broken-down cars in the front yard.

Between us and South Mountain, we could see nothing but the bluish glow and the ripple of the mirage that seemed to hang over all of pre-boom Phoenix, then more desert before Mexico.

And Crazy Willie's dumb old Missouri-born father had found a way for us to "make a boot-load of money" on weekends.

Scrapper Jack, Duke, and Armando were forced by finances and the size of their families to listen to him, so we kids were rustled out of bed around 5:30 a.m. on a

Saturday morning in November.

Big Willie's '52 Plymouth sat idling outside our door next to Duke's '50 Ford pickup, and we piled in. Young Armando's cousins, who had stayed over, came too, so there were about ten of us kids.

One of the cousins was named Jesus (but you pronounced it Hey-zoos). He had brought apples, so we had them for breakfast.

Some kids scrambled into the back of the pickup, but four of us were in the car.

Adults got the car seats, so we scrunched up on the floor, leaned against the rear of the front seat, knees pulled up to our chins, eating apples. Although I didn't know the term "irony," I knew there was something funny about Jesus bringing us apples.

The vibration of the floorboards kept us nearly asleep, heads bobbing, faces sweating and nowhere to put the finished apple cores, until we got to the fields.

As we drove, Jesus told us the story of the other name for the mountains south of our new place. It was called Superstition Mountain, and Jesus said it was watched over by a band of dead Apaches.

"An old German guy found gold in the mountain, but he got run off by some Apaches. They might of killed him right in the mine, but I think they runned him off.

It don't matter cuz he wasn't the real owner of the mine. The gold belonged to our leader. It wasn't really a mine but a place where the Mexican leader hid his gold. The Apaches were always fighting with us, and they found the gold. A band of human beings were told to guard the gold, and they did until they died. No one knows who killed them, but now everyone who finds the Lost Dutchman's Mine gets killed. Some people say it is the spirits of the Apache guards who kill them. My uncle says it's the Dutchman. I don't know, but it seems it might be either. Don't matter who killed you if you're dead, right?"

When we got to the cotton fields, the boss made us sit in the sun for a time made longer because I didn't speak Spanish, and then Jesus' sister Rosi told me it was to let the dew on the cotton dry so it would be lighter.

After the wait, we slung the straps of the white canvas bags over our shoulders and headed off between the rows of child-sized cotton plants. The bags were about five times my length and heavy and getting heavier as you filled them up with cotton. In the cotton field, life got more difficult the more you did what you were supposed to do.

"No sticks, no pods, no seeds," the boss shouted after us.

Cotton picked for a buck per hundred pounds didn't

amount to a "boot load" of money for any of us. But Rosi said it was plenty for them.

I asked why, and she said "Well," then stopped, and I could tell she was about to tell me something she wasn't supposed to. She assessed her family a few rows off, recanted and settled for, "Well, because we're different."

At lunch, my mother and father sat with Armando and Rosalita and Armando's brother and his wife and laughed while we kids chased a white dog through the fields.

The afternoon was oppressive and long. My neck was burnt, and my fingers, where the nail joins the meat, were sliced bloody from the dried pods not wanting to give up their clutch of cotton, and my lower back stung sweet with the strain of bending.

Together we lost our will to play in the sun-clenched late afternoon of an Arizona cotton field.

At the end of the day, I dragged the ever heavier, long canvas bag along the rows to the payout station. All the men stood and watched as I pulled the bag onto the scale. As I got some of it on the scale on one side, the other side would fall off, but as hot as I was, I dragged and nudged the damn thing until it was on. The boss squinted at the numbers.

"Seventy-five pounds," he said.

I stood waiting for my seventy-five cents when he said. "You have to have a hundred pounds to get paid. Next."

I didn't move. My insides wanted to cry, but my outside said, "Don't you dare." I stood staring at him. He returned my stare for what seemed to be a long time. Then suddenly he took seventy-five cents from the metal payout box and handed it to me. I took my money and turned to find a very large black man standing behind me staring over top of me at the boss. I guess that's why I got paid. As I walked by the big man who had stood behind me, he patted me on the shoulder.

"Good job," he said.

On the ride home, Marta, young Armando's little sister, slept leaning on my shoulder, and I was embarrassed at how I must have smelled, but I guess she smelled the same way.

The cousins didn't return with us. Instead, they loaded into a crowded canvas-covered truck. I stood with my mother and father, who seemed sad, and we waved to them as the truck rolled off down the dirt road south.

"Where are they going?" I asked.

"Home," my mother said, wiping the blood from her knuckles with hardened fingers.

There were things I didn't understand in that cotton field. I didn't understand why weekends sometimes meant work, because other kids my age who went to Rio Vista didn't have jobs. And I didn't understand why my mother was so sad to say goodbye to that family, because she had only just met them today.

We had all baked and sweated and played together in the fields — Mexicans, Americans, and Texans — and I didn't know why Rosi would tell me we were different, because… well, because we just plain weren't.

Chapter Six
Finding Fortitude
November

My mother laughed one morning when I asked her, "Do I really have to go to school?"

"You're darn right," she said. "Are you wearing underwear?"

I reached into my pants and made believe I was checking. "Yes," I said.

"Then you're going to school."

It had been the end of November, and the sixth-grade class was already two months into its school year when I arrived. On that first day, I stood in the office of the principal with my mother. I never knew the name of the principal; nobody told me. I guess I was just supposed to shut up and listen. I was in a place where I really had no idea about anything, and I was being introduced to Mr. Chai, who was to be my teacher. He was Chinese, so I wondered if he was Jewish. Everyone spoke English up front, but the undercurrent in the background conversation was in Spanish.

The building was a sprawling one-story affair. Each classroom had a front and back door, both emptied into the open air. There was no air conditioning, and the nearly ninety-degree heat meant we would spend as much time outside on the expansive fields and playgrounds. Lunch sometimes lasted for two hours. I guess they figured they couldn't teach us anything if they didn't first keep us alive.

The first few weeks had been uneventful, except that I realized St. Mary's school in the fifth grade was way ahead of Rio Vista in the sixth grade.

I didn't understand much about the tension between some of the white kids and the Mexican kids, but I understood poverty. Most of us at Rio Vista understood that. It was our common ground.

After the first few weeks of school, I spent several days taking an interest in one girl in my class.

With her steel-gray eyes and long, dirty-blonde hair, Johna-Jean was easily the best-looking girl in the school and probably in the entire city. She was from Oklahoma.

It seemed no white person in Phoenix came from here originally, only the Mexicans and Indians. I always thought it was fitting that her exquisite appearance made up for the fact that her family was poorer than mine, which meant they had nothing. In the morning, sitting in class waiting for school to start, I sometimes watched her walk around the room. She was well-liked and meandered from desk to desk, talking and laughing.

But today, I had also been watching Patricia, a frail, pale, nice enough looking girl with wispy brown hair who sat two seats down from me and one row to the right.

Patricia was extracting things from her red purse. First, she put her Paper-Mate fountain pen in the tray on the top of her desk. Then she put her lunch quarter on the corner, pulled out her round mother-of-pearl mirror and held it by the handle up to her face. She adjusted her hair, and then I saw her pale blue eyes in the glass just for a second.

I liked Patricia because she had the same name as my oldest sister who didn't come with us to Arizona. I missed my sister, so the name made me feel good when the roll was called.

Ross, a big Mexican kid who was quickly becoming one of my best friends, got to sell the lunch tickets because no one would dare try to grab an extra from Ross.

Mr. Chai called the class to order, and Johna-Jean walked down the aisle toward her seat. As she passed Patricia's desk, she placed her hand on the quarter. One more step and the quarter disappeared.

Ross started down the first aisle selling tickets, and Patricia began to look around, first on her desk, then on the floor. With every step Ross took, Patricia's panic grew.

I saw Johna-Jean out of the corner of my eye. She watched the search widen its radius.

When Ross got to Patricia's desk, she told him what happened. He started to give her a ticket, but she stood up and shouted, "No!"

Tears of frustration covered her face. "Someone stole my quarter. I had it here." She pointed to the corner of the desk.

Mr. Chai asked if anyone had seen the coin on the desk.

I raised my hand. "It was there." I said, pointing.

Mr. Chai had Ross sit down with the tickets.

"Okay," said the teacher. "No one does anything else until Patricia gets her lunch money back."

Dead silence.

We all searched around the room and, trying not to be too pointed, I glanced at Johna-Jean. She stared out the window, and she too had tears in her eyes. I wondered what the nuns of my first five years of education would want me to do. I stood up, walked to Patricia's desk and put my quarter on the corner. I leaned down and whispered something to her.

She assessed me, then turned to Mr. Chai, and she said, "He didn't take it."

"Did you?" the teacher asked.

"I didn't take it," I said, and I sat back down. There seemed to be a sudden chill in the morning air.

"Who did?"

Patricia sat mute. So did I. So did Johna-Jean. Faced with a protracted problem or getting on with the day, Mr. Chai motioned for Ross to go ahead with the tickets.

As he passed my desk, Ross tore off a ticket and dropped it on the floor.

At lunch, Johna-Jean sat with me, and in a muffled tone, looking directly at her food, she said, "Thanks."

"It's okay," I answered.

I understood poor. I stared right in its face most of my life, and I knew that when you get the hungries you get the stupids. I knew this girl wasn't a thief, just hungry. Patricia knew it too, and neither of us wanted to hurt Johna-Jean any further than life already had. And Ross knew, at eleven years old, what I had done was a good thing, and he took it into his own hands to make it right.

Mr. Chai had just let life happen. No harm, no foul. A tough Mexican kid, a rich white girl, a couple of trailer park urchins, and a Chinese elementary school teacher in a southwestern desert had felt enough empathy and understanding for one another to make the best of a bad situation. For that group of people it had been the natural thing to do.

That afternoon, I found Posey in the schoolyard. He was destroying someone at tetherball. I waited, sitting in the grass until the destruction was complete. He came and sat beside me.

"Hey, do you guys go to church?" I asked.

"Who?"

"You and Garrett. Do you go to church?"

"Why?"

"There's nothing to do on Sunday, you know, except watch Ned butcher cows. I was just thinking we should go to church. I used to go all the time. I just thought we might go."

"Okay, I'll find out where we can go," Posey said. He broke his Baby Ruth bar in half and handed part to me.

"Have you ever had Dr. Pepper?" he asked.

"What's that?"

"It's soda pop. C'mon," he said and jumped to his feet.

I followed him across the yard to the cafeteria, where there were three vending machines. Posey went to the one in the middle and turned to see who was watching. When he saw no one was paying attention to us, he stepped around behind the machine and plugged it in. He hit the coin return, and enough money came back for me to buy my first Dr. Pepper.

So on the next Sunday, Posey, Garrett, Johna-Jean, and I went to church.

Posey had learned from Johna-Jean that, in her world, weekends were for making a few bucks, and religion was part of that. Some religions would pay a quarter for each new person you brought in, so one of us would go into places like "The Reverend Keester's Church of Life and Mental Reservations" one week, and "Our Lady of Perpetual Motion" the next. The deal must have been, if the kids came one week, maybe the adults would come the next week, and they would drop more than a quarter into the donation box.

Instead of bringing parents the next week, we would bring the other kids, collect our reverse tithe, stay a half-hour or so, and then go on to the next religion.

After a few weeks of this, one of the preachers found out where we lived, walked to the house on a Monday, and told my mother I had been thrown out of his church and wasn't welcome back. Mum calmly told me she would kill me if I ever got thrown out of church again. A few Sundays later, Posey brought us to a new church.

The minister met us at the door, and when we pretty much held out our hands for the money, he put us off.

"After the service," he said abruptly, and walked back into the dark, hot room full of benches.

Inside, there were only four or five drunks, some old ladies, a young couple, and one Mexican family who seemed lost and unsure if they were in the right place.

While his sermon droned on about how, "There must be a hell because scientists have proven the center of the earth is molten lava," I noticed a stack of cases of Dr. Pepper next to the soda machine. I elbowed Johna-Jean and pointed at it with my nose.

Garrett had found something even more interesting. In the corner was a row of candles, and at the end was a tin box.

The preacher rambled on, and pretty soon he was even belittling those people who, as he said, "would come to services just for money. To give is the way to the Lord's heart. The Lord needs to have more money than the devil so he can buy a better world."

I felt a quick chill and told the others, "He's gonna stiff us."

I got up, walked across the room, and leaned against the soda machine.

Posey and Garrett scooched down the bench to the end near the candles, and Johna-Jean sat in the middle where the minister could see her very plainly. Even though she was in my class, it turned out she was thirteen. I figured that was why she was built like my sister Diane.

When we were certain the minister was pretty much fixed on her short shorts, I filled my pockets and belt with bottles of soda, while Garrett emptied the tin box.

Like a donkey caught between two equally accessible carrots, the preacher stood still, his mouth open in a weird smile, as we all turned and bolted for the door.

There, filling the door, was the biggest man I had ever seen, in a white shirt the size of a tent. And he wasn't budging. All I could think of was, "Ma is going to kill me if I get thrown out of church again."

I ignored the real danger of arrest or worse. He didn't know my name yet, and I wasn't about to let him find out. We raced into the back hall, searching for a whiff of outside air or a glint of sunlight to follow. To the right was a bathroom. The preacher and the other guy started down the hall after us, followed by part of the congregation. We pushed the door open and rushed into the men's room. Johna-Jean giggled as we stepped inside.

An open window gaped at us, but it was small and high above one of the stalls.

"Ma's going to kill me," I heard myself say. I stepped on the toilet, up onto the roll holder, to the top of the partition — I reached across to a hanging pipe and swung out the window.

Outside, I grabbed Garrett's feet and pulled him out, then Posey, and then we all helped Johna-Jean.

Somehow we had done it.

The preacher never did get a chance to say, "Ah thank ah'll jes call yo-ah parents." But in the back of the building, a mean-looking dog hung from a rope that was tied to a lower branch of a tree. The dog had been forced to bite the end of the rope to hold on. We were outside the church, but now we had to outrun this dog to the fence, the street and safety. Later, Posey told me that was how bad guys trained dogs to fight in the pit. It strengthened their jaws.

We had stolen money from a donation box, made off with six sodas, didn't fall from the window eight feet to the cement floor, and as we sprinted away trying to make it to the fence before the canine monster tore us up, all I could think of was, "It's a good thing, because Ma would have killed me if I got thrown out of church again."

From then on, I wrote off going to church as my job

and decided we would have to find another way to make money. The soda machine was a good idea. We would unplug all the ones outside markets, bus stations, and of course the one at school, and then plug them back in later in the afternoon and collect other people's change.

After a few days of that, we decided we might be able to do something similar to the phone booths that dotted the city around us. This turned out to be a good source of dimes, nickels, and sometimes quarters. Each public phone had a coin return. It was an opening where money would drop if the coin return button at the top of the phone was pushed. We stuffed paper up inside the opening. At the end of the day we would make the rounds to each public pay phone, pull out the plug of paper, and the change from the day would fall down. Then we would move on to the next booth.

With that money, and with the two-cent deposit on each empty bottle we would collect from the shelves inside the markets and turn in at the courtesy booth, we had enough money to keep us in candy, yo-yos, marbles, fish hooks, cigarettes, and the like.

One day, I noticed that the bottles we turned in were put in a wooden case, and, when it was full, one of the store employees would take it out to the rear of the store and leave it on the loading dock to be picked up... so we picked them up, and, a few at a time, we brought them to the deposit register. It was almost too easy. Every day we turned in the same bottles and got different money.

Some days we could make a few dollars at a time when my father made only about fifty bucks a week.

The nuns had always told me that God would provide. I convinced myself that this was how He did it.

One afternoon when I returned to our place from a day of such entrepreneurship, I found my father sitting on the front stoop with Diane. They had obviously been discussing something that they had to be done discussing because of my arrival.

"Is that okay with you?" he asked her.

"I suppose so," she answered, stood up, and went back into the house.

Scrapper Jack rose slowly and caught the eye of my mother, who was sitting inside the window. He said, "I'm going to go talk to him now." She nodded at him.

Duke appeared out of the darkness. The two men exchanged a meaningful glance and began to walk down the line of apartments.

It seemed a guy Diane had met on the bus trip from Milford and had sat with most of the way, had found her, and he had even rented the last apartment in our building.

I followed the two men.

"Where do you think you're going?" Dad asked.

"With you, okay?"

He stopped for a few seconds, looked down at me, and then surprisingly said, "Sure, why not?"

He knocked on the door to the apartment. I saw the guy peek out the window and hesitate.

"It's alright, son. I just want to talk to you," my father said.

The guy opened the door, walked into the living room, and sat down on his couch.

Duke stood just inside the door. Dad pulled a kitchen chair from the table and sat backwards on it only a few feet from the man who I figured was in his twenties. He had a DA hairdo, which was popular back then. It was called that because it was combed around the sides of the head, and it resembled a duck's ass from the back.

"Your name is Robert?" Dad asked, and the guy nodded.

"Do ya know who I am?"

The man nodded again.

"You know why I'm here, Robert?"

He nodded again.

"This is how I see it, Robert," he said. "You're what, twenty-three, twenty-four?"

"Twenty-four."

"You seem like a good kid. I don't blame you for noticing her. She doesn't seem to be fifteen, does she?"

"No, sir, she sure don't."

"But she is." My father stood up and looked down at the young man. His smile disappeared. "So, you being a good kid and all, and her not seeming to be fifteen, I sure wouldn't want to have to kill you, so I think you should go away somewhere. What do you think, Robert?"

"I think so, sir."

Did my father just threaten to kill someone? Damned if he didn't. And I was worried about a few cases of deposit bottles being a sin. All I could think of on the walk to our apartment was what about the commandment, *thou shalt not kill?* It occurred to me almost immediately that the commandment didn't say anything about not *threatening* to kill.

The next day, that end apartment was empty, and I had a new vision of Scrapper Jack Hourihan.

I was getting further and further away from being the kid who had been taught by nuns. I wondered if I would ever get back to who I had been when family and religion were the two most important influences in my life, and Jesus, Mary, and Joseph were as real a presence as anyone else in my family. As we walked to our own place that night, we didn't speak. The reality of life was beginning to consistently supersede the spirituality of religion. It seemed to me that the further we got from St. Mary's, the more easily we could find acceptable alternatives to the Ten Commandments.

Toward the end of the week at school, I decided I needed to do something about Donny.

Donny was proud that he was the king of mule, and pride will make you do things you shouldn't, like taking all Johna-Jean's marbles. He should have left her some.

Mule is a marble game conceived by someone who had more marbles than everyone else. But it's a good way to lose all those marbles in the twenty minutes between getting to school and first bell. It is the lure of shooting one marble and quickly getting four in return that coaxed the lines full every morning. You can stand for all of history and watch everyone else throw all their marbles away one after the other until their bags are emptied, but you will still believe you are the one who can ultimately win it.

Early in the morning, before the desert sun would stoke up and brand reality into the tops of our heads and send us scurrying inside, we set up the game. Eight or ten mule skinners sat in front of the cafeteria building and leaned back against the cool hard brick, spreading our legs into a vulnerable pose and setting up a triangle of marbles in the grass.

The mule marble was then balanced on top of the triangle. About ten paces away, a line of shooters would form. The object: To knock down the mule with one shot, thus winning it.

If you miss, the mule skinner keeps your marble.

The trick is to get low, almost like bowling, and pinch-nut your marble with your thumb, off your two forefingers, along the ground, and knock over the mule. Even in this form, it is a game that favors the house.

Each school morning during marble season, I would show up early and set up a mule.

Each day I won. Unless Donny was shooting.

He, as I stated earlier, was the king of mule, the last remaining superpower at Rio Vista Elementary School. This morning, he had taken all my neighbors' mules and waited at the end of my line, flipping an aggie and smiling. Donny had decimated most of my friends, but when he took all of Johna-Jean's marbles, I decided something had to be done.

This morning I was ready for him.

When it was his turn, he eyed my marble pyramid, took a quick step, bent and skimmed a cat's eye along the ground, straight at my mule.

I reached out front and caught it.

Everyone was stunned. You just didn't do that.

"What's the matter," I shouted, "can't you shoot mule standing up?"

Everyone laughed.

"Stand-up mule? That's just crazy," he said.

"Not good enough?" I asked.

So he summoned his bravado and faced me. Standing up, you would have to hit the mule from the air, or careen into it on the bounce. Now, odds were not just against the shooter, but nearing impossible.

Donny lost his marbles trying to win at stand-up mule. I gave them to Johna-Jean.

He should have left my friends alone.

Chapter Seven

Fear of the Lord, and Freddie
December

For the first time in my life, we didn't go to church on Christmas. It shook me. I kept waiting for Mum to say, "Okay, let's get dressed and go to Mass," but it was late morning, and it hadn't happened yet.

Dennis and Neil were outside in shorts and t-shirts, playing cowboys and Indians beside the ditch in the middle of the winter. Garrett, Posey, and I were playing a game of throwing knives at each other's feet to see how close to the foot we could get without sticking each other. We did this barefoot, otherwise it would just be not worth doing. While Posey threw at my foot, I noticed a trickle of water beginning to wet the dry dirt of the irrigation ditch beside us. Soon we would be able to collect crayfish, or "crawdads" as the kids from Tennessee called them.

All the kids were outside. We were all dressed in shorts and t-shirts, except for Tim and Danny Boy's older cousin DeDe, who wore shorts and a halter top because she had stuff she was trying not to hide. We used to like to play "piggy-back" where one kid got on another kid's back and raced, or "chicken fighting," where each kid got piggy-back on another kid, and you tried to knock each other over. In either of these games, if you were fortunate enough to get on DeDe's back, you also got to reach around and feel her breasts. She never said anything about it. It added another level to the enjoyment of the game.

When the ditch began to fill up, it became the center of interest for most of the kids.

I turned and went inside. I had to see the Christmas tree. I had to see the ornaments. They weren't our ornaments. There was no religion in them at all. We had bought them at the market. They were Santa and snowmen and round colored balls. The tree was devoid of crosses or miniature statues of the sacred heart of Jesus. But we had the cooked ham, sitting on the counter waiting to be heated. I thought, "At least we are having ham."

I was happy to have nearly my whole family with me. I missed Patty, but strangely, I suddenly also missed my Aunt Kathleen, Gram, and my cousins. It was Christmas, we weren't all getting together at Gram's house, and it fell on me like a heavy, cold cloud. My life would never be the same. My religion had deserted me, or I had deserted it. Either way, half of me seemed to have died, and Christmas made me recognize it.

I went back outside. My father had gone to the Silver Dollar for a beer with Duke, but my mother sat on the front steps with my sisters, who had dragged kitchen chairs into a semi-circle around her while she peeled potatoes. Dennis and Neil were now sitting at the edge of the ditch with their feet in the water.

"Watch for snakes," Mum called to them. They nodded.

With my family outside, it was surprising when the door to the apartment opened from the inside.

The little girl from the family who had moved in to fill the place abandoned by Robert stepped out of our apartment. She was about three years old and small, with skinny legs that bulged at the knees, and arms that bulged at the elbows. Her shoulder length, blonde curls were dirty and clumped, her dress was stained by grease, and her huge blue eyes peered at us suspiciously over our ham that she held in two hands, one at each end of the bone, and she was gnawing away at it. She must have gone in the back door and took it off the counter.

I was horrified.

My sisters laughed, my mother smiled, and I stepped forward to retrieve the ham.

"No," my mother said. "Leave her alone. She's hungry."

She turned to the little girl. "Would you like something to drink with that?" she asked.

The little girl nodded without stopping her carnivorous attack on what was to have been our Christmas dinner.

My mother got up from the step and went in to get a glass of apple juice.

"What are we going to eat?" I asked. We were all laughing.

"We'll find something. She's hungry. Let her eat."

I thought, "I'm hungry too." No presents, no snow, no Jesus, no church, and now this. I was amazed and proud of my mother and really pissed off that we were now not even going to have ham for Christmas.

The twins and I were sent to the store to buy Kraft Dinner and hot dogs. We walked to the Bayless Supermarket, and as we approached it, a young woman ran by us. The manager stepped from the front door and shouted, "Stop her! She's a thief." Sheila and I stood on the sidewalk, not knowing what to do. Nancy bolted after the woman.

Not long ago, black and white were still the only division in our world. Things then were still either a sin or not a sin. Since we had arrived here, there had become so many shades of gray. Our father worked at the market, so it was sort of our place the woman had stolen from. Nancy was much faster and wasn't carrying anything. She caught the woman, and as I caught up, I saw that the woman clutched bread and milk. Nancy too had noticed what had been "stolen." She assessed the young woman. We turned back to see the manager walking toward us. Nancy turned to the woman and said, "Run, he can't catch you."

The manager reached us as the woman turned the corner of the building and sped off through a field.

He asked Nancy, "Why did you let her go?"

"She wasn't stealing," my sister said. "She was feeding someone."

We bought what we had been sent for and returned home.

When we got to the end of South Second Street, across the dirt expanse in front of me, I saw Posey and Garrett walking from their front door with their baseball gloves.

"You coming?" Posey called to me. I nodded, bolted

into the house for my glove, and followed them.

"Don't miss supper," my mother called. "In case we have one." She laughed, and we were off to play baseball — on Christmas. The entire world had turned a corner.

Posey and Garrett weren't great baseball players. They weren't even passable good. Actually, they were horrible. Everyone let them play because they didn't want Posey to beat the crap out of them. On the other hand, I could hit, and I could pitch. We spent the afternoon in a very high scoring game of close plays, no umpires, and a lot of fights. Being able to fight was just as important as being able to field a ground ball in a pick-up baseball game in South Phoenix. When it was nearly time for possible supper, we began our trek across the desert to home.

Freddie was a shaved-head Mexican kid who believed Phoenix was his country, which was pretty much true. We white kids were foreigners, since Freddie's ancestors had lived right here when it was still Mexico. It wasn't as if they had crossed a border. It was more that the border had crossed them.

Freddie, at twelve years old, was the same size as Posey and had already won several prize fights. I usually went along with him, whatever he said. I had learned that discretion was also the better part of self-preservation.

Freddie charged up from behind.

"Hey, chico, that's my glove you got there," he said as he caught up. We all turned to face him.

He pointed at a first-baseman's mitt in Garrett's hand. Posey extended his hand to his younger brother, palm up. He wiggled his fingers, and Garrett smiled and handed the glove to his big brother.

I knew neither brother owned a first baseman's mitt, so I figured Freddie was telling the truth.

I quietly told Posey, "Give it back."

"I don't see y'all's name on it." Posey said, and I shuddered. Posey turned the glove over in his hand, "Nope, no name."

Freddie was tough, but it was a tough neighborhood all around, and there were more of us than him at the moment.

"See you at school," he said, and his gaze took in not only Posey but all three of us.

Posey smiled, enjoying his moment of numerical superiority.

On the Monday after the holiday vacation, I should have begged off school and stayed behind. Posey had bitten off more than he could chew, and I knew if I went I would be in the middle of it, but I always walked to school with the Texans and the two boys from Tennessee.

Halfway to school, there was a fenced-in field, about fifty-yards square, which contained a bull. Where we climbed into the field, an irrigation ditch paralleled the fence. It left a four-foot path to walk on, and the ditch kept us safe from the bull.

We took our first few steps into the field. I saw Freddie and his friends climb over the other end of the fence on the same side of the ditch.

Posey turned to the rest of us. "Don't show 'em you're ascared," he said, and he walked directly toward Freddie and his five friends.

I knew that listening to the strategy of the guy whose stupidity had gotten us into this in the first place was not a good idea, but there I went, walking up beside him, all celluloid tough, like we were in a movie. A few steps later, intelligence overtook me. I turned and asked the Nashville twins, "You know anything about bulls?"

"Sure," Tim said. "If you run in their field, they'll chase you down and pummel your ass."

"Come on, walk this way," I said. "Don't nobody run." I hopped the ditch and started walking cross-wise across the field toward the other side, perpendicular to the direction we had been walking. The bull stood in the middle, eating grass and eyeing us curiously. We walked on slowly. Freddie realized if we got to the other side before him, we would get lost in the traffic on the big road and get away, so he and his friends made a bad mistake. They started running across the field after us.

"Keep walking," I said. We did, and the bull turned, stomped, and the last thing I saw was Freddie and his friends running for their lives with a bull close behind.

That Wednesday, Posey brought the glove to school and gave it back to Freddie. It hadn't actually belonged to Freddie either. It belonged to his little cousin.

"We should'a jes let 'em fight it out," Posey laughed. Freddie laughed, and detente was re-established. Before he walked away from the summit meeting, Freddie winked at me. He knew I had talked Posey into giving it back. He probably also knew the bull was my idea. Posey and I walked off with his arm around my shoulder. I had become best friends… with both of them.

That afternoon when I got home from school, there was something wrong. As I turned into the drive in front of our house, I saw Nancy running into DeDe's apartment. Right behind her was Crazy Willie's father. As I got a little closer, I saw smoke coming out of the kitchen window.

I decided Nancy might need help, so I went in too. Nancy was at the stove, and a fire poured like a dragon's breath out of a pan on one of the burners. Willie's old man decided he should be in charge as I got closer to the problem.

"Throw some water on it!" he shouted.

Nancy grabbed a second pot and filled it with water.

"Throw it on there!" he shouted again.

So she did, and the grease fire climbed up the wall and spread from burning in the pot to the wall and up the side of the cupboard.

Willie's father shoved Nancy out of the way and nearly ran right over me trying to get out of the house.

Nancy, not so calmly, picked up the cover of the original pot and covered it. The fire went out, and the wall was once again visible. It was going out by itself. As we walked out the front door, we saw my mother standing with some firemen next to a fire truck. Funny thing was that firefighters didn't work the same way in Arizona as they did in Massachusetts. They arrived and checked the house for a fire plaque. Despite seeing the fire, they told my mother they couldn't do anything about it, "Since y'all don't have fire insurance."

Chapter Eight
Piety Be Damned
January

My Irish-Catholic, New England-born family was becoming unrecognizable.

My father drank heavily when he wasn't working. Who could say he didn't have a reason? Diane enjoyed life a little too much. Nancy and Sheila were bribing her to keep her secrets. Dennis climbed inside himself. Neil watched it all too closely. I organized a group of thieves that would have rivaled that of Fegin's pickpockets in Oliver Twist, and Mum was losing control.

My mother had taken a job at Jay's Frozen Dessert Company. She filled quart boxes with soft-serve ice milk, froze it in the most wonderful walk-in freezer ever designed, and conducted the distribution of it to every market and restaurant in the Phoenix area. She was the entire workforce of the company.

With my father away all day in the produce department of a Bayless market and my mother away at Jay's, we kids began to have free rein. Diane at fifteen, Nancy and Sheila at thirteen, myself at ten, Dennis at eight and Neil at seven… we were pretty much on our own, living in a barrio in a city that was still part of the Wild West.

One January morning, I boarded the city bus with Diane. The twins were in charge of Dennis and Neil at home. My parents were at work, and a free bus ride all over the city was cheap entertainment.

We sat in the front seat across the aisle from the bus driver. Diane and the driver, a middle-aged redhead, gazed intently through the rearview mirror, lost in each other's eyes. I wondered how he could drive without knowing what traffic was behind him, or, for that matter, in front of him. After a long ride, the bus stopped at the public transportation depot. The driver went inside. Diane stood and told me to stay in the seat. "We'll be headed out pretty soon," she said.

I waited in my seat. She waited outside the door in the shade of a small date palm tree.

After a few minutes, the driver stepped out of the

door, turned to my sister, and I could have sworn he kissed her. I started protectively out of my seat, but I realized she didn't seem to be in any trouble. She wasn't resisting at all. He was about the age of my father, and I was confused.

She returned to the seat. She gave me a look that said, "Don't even open your mouth." He stepped onto the bus and smiled at her, returned to the driver's seat, and began our trip back into South Phoenix.

I walked with her in silence from the bus stop to our apartment, and I was horrified when she placed a nickel each in the hands of her sisters. They were being paid to keep their mouths shut about their sister, who was only two years older than they were and who had been sent to Arizona to be our mother. Now, she had a secret boyfriend who, it turned out, had five kids in his own marriage. She had been turned loose from mommy duty when Sheila arrived, since it had always been Sheila's job to "watch the kids." Nancy spent time riding horses at a neighbor's house and blackmailing her older sister for candy money. One day, the neighbor brought a colt to the house and asked Nancy if she wanted to ride it. With my mother's reluctant permission, my sister climbed aboard the young horse. It began bucking. She held on. It jumped the ditch and the fence. She hung on. It bolted through a neighbor's porch, knocking over patio furniture. She wouldn't let go. Finally the horse quieted down, the man got hold of the reins, and Nancy climbed off. The horse, before that morning, had never been ridden.

We Hourihan kids were nothing if we were not adept at holding on. My sister had broken a horse. We were definitely in the Wild West.

The day of the bus ride, when Diane and I got home, something was going on. According to Sheila, Posey had punched Dennis, taken his baseball glove, and wouldn't give it back. Since Diane and I were gone, it fell on Nancy's shoulders to get it back. The next day I got the story from Tim. "Your sister just asked for the glove, and Posey laughed at her, so she damn near broke his arm, picked up the glove where he had dropped it, and she walked off home. Posey ran home. Nancy just grabbed his arm and shoved it up his back until he cried and dropped the glove," Tim said. I guess Garrett and Posey had a thing about taking other people's baseball gloves. I guess I should have told them about my big sister.

Chapter Nine

Fear of God

February

Dennis and Neil seemed lost. Dennis was lost in guilt, and Neil in the chaos of this new family. Before they had even become comfortable on Purchase Street, we had moved. Just when Pine Street had become home, they were put on a bus and sent across the country. And I was not doing anything to help them.

It was during February when fishing became the thing to do. I went with Posey to the main irrigation canal south of us, down by the dentist's office. We returned with some smallish catfish. My brothers had been catching crayfish in the ditch and had about fifteen or so in a bucket.

Neil was not real happy with them since one of them

had pinched him on the finger. He was poking a stick into the bucket until one would latch on and then he'd pull it out. Cindy, DeDe's little sister, watched him.

"Careful, Neil," she said as he started to pull the little lobster off the stick. "He'll painchou."

"What?" Neil asked.

"He'll paint chu."

"What?" Neil was laughing.

"Painchu, painchu. He'll painchu." Cindy was not laughing. She frowned at him. This boy, who was at least two or three years her junior, was laughing at her. She was not happy.

"He'll paint me? I don't think so." Neil's sense of humor had arrived even at seven years old. "He doesn't have a brush."

Cindy grew more and more frustrated. "He will painch yew," she pronounced carefully.

"Oh. He'll pinch me?"

"Raht," Cindy answered.

"He already did," Neil said, and showed her his middle finger with the pinched tip.

While we laughed, Dennis sat down at the steps and cleaned and filleted the fish, took it inside, and fried it. In the time since we had arrived in Phoenix, Denny had become quieter almost each day. None of us ever said anything about why we were in this desert, but it seemed that Dennis knew why we were here, and he wasn't happy about it. Most of the time he sat on the couch watching us as if we were a TV show that he wasn't part of.

The twins, Nancy and Sheila, were going to South Mountain High. Sheila, who was quiet, was being picked on for being the new Yankee white girl. Every day at school the mostly not-white kids would chant at her "Bahston, Bahston, Bahston," and they would walk up behind her and step on her shoe backs until it was difficult for her to walk. No one picked on Nancy more than once.

I guess the difference I saw in my twin sisters was evident when, on their fourteenth birthday, Sheila overheard Duke saying he was going to give them their birthday spanking. She quietly, smartly, got comfortable in the closet, and Nancy bravely faced him and outran him until he gave up and went home. Of course, when Nancy finally came home, Duke bolted out of his door and caught her. He spanked her fourteen times with a belt.

Each day, no matter how much bullying there was, the twins walked to school. Nancy took the shortcut across a plank laid across a pretty wide irrigation canal. Sheila walked the extra couple of hundred feet to the bridge.

It was hard for me to figure out which one of them was right.

And me?

It was inevitable. Without the guidance of family, friends, and the fear of God, or at least fear of Sister Mary Patrick, I enjoyed a stint on the bad side of the law.

The first thing I learned was it is better to be the brains of the outfit than it is to be the other end.

Scrapper Jack himself was proud of his boy (me) the night everyone else's kids were arrested for a shoplifting endeavor that the store manager said was the "best thought-out plan" he had ever seen not work.

For weeks before it happened, Posey and Garrett, Tim and Danny Boy from Tennessee, Crazy Willie from Missouri, and I met at the junk yard every few days, pestered the pit bull with sticks, played some Blackjack, shot marbles, played catch, or went to the supermarket across the big street to steal candy and cigarettes.

Inside the door, to the left, were the registers and the main store. To the right was the candy row. Perpendicular to others, it was wedged between the front plate-glass window and the courtesy booth, and pretty much untouchable because you could be seen from everywhere, but there were some candy bars in the general part of the store too.

The really big adult–sized Hershey bars were up the center aisle with the baking goods, so every few days we would grab one or two of those and stuff them in our pants, skirt the cash registers, and speed out the door.

We never got caught, but I saw a problem. And, as I told them all after a game of kick-the-can one night, "It's just too easy," and we could only get Hershey bars.

I explained, "We all go inside the front door." I stopped for effect, like the bad guys on TV. "Everyone but Tim and Danny Boy. You two wait outside. Then, while we wait in the candy aisle, you go in arguing and go right in front of the registers so everyone sees you. You gotta make them believe." I paused again. "Then Danny Boy here whacks you in the mouth in the pickle aisle." "What?" Tim asked. It sounded as if he hadn't been listening until here.

"Remember when those two redneck kids had a fight the other day? Think about what happened."

What had happened was the courtesy booth had emptied, the cashiers all ran down to stop the fight, and the manager went with them because they were in the pickle aisle, and that could get messy if the jars started breaking.

I told them how the rest of us would just hang around in front near the Coke machine.

"Then you two start whaling on each other."

This was no problem, since the two cousins were always whaling on each other for one thing or another. I attributed it to them being brought up in the hills of Tennessee before the whole family rustled themselves out to Phoenix.

"Then when everyone goes running to the fight, we fill up our shirts and just run like hell out the front door, big as life. What do you think?"

"Sounds great," Posey said, "When do we do it?"

"Tomorrow afternoon," I said

There was one hitch in my plan. Coach had called an unscheduled baseball practice, and I forgot all about the plan. I should have known something was up when Willie didn't show up for practice, but I didn't think about it. My team practiced until dusk, and I came home to a darkened house.

All the parents and all the kids were at Duke's. I could see them all in the window, and it didn't appear promising. My father saw me and called me inside.

Posey's father did the honors.

"Y'all done a bad thing, heah. You jes don't steal stuff. It ain't right. An ya don't get caught cuz that's jes stupid."

Posey gave me his "shut up" look.

"Now, the police say they'll leave this to us, but we

gonna have ta punish all y'all. No fishing. No candy. No television. No baseball."

No baseball? Crazy Willie and I were the only ones on the team. This was too much punishment. Then Duke, seeing my reaction, said, "Not you Li'l Boston. You ain't gonna be punished. You wasn't there."

My father put his arm around my shoulder and said, "Well, don't be too hard on them, Duke. C'mon Johnny, let's go home."

As he told me over the kitchen table how proud he was when the cops called, and then brought the whole passel of kids home, and I wasn't there, my mother raised an eyebrow, smiled, and shook her head.

I learned something else that night about being on the wrong side of the law, and I told the others the next day. "It ain't my fault," I said. "You should know better than to go along with a plan that ends, 'and then run like hell.'"

Nobody squealed.

A few days later, we broke into a house down the street from us. I grabbed a brand-new flashlight from the place, and Posey took a hunting knife. Only a day or so later, Duke saw my brand-new flashlight that was just like his, only his was old and beat up.

"Ah tell you what, L'il Boston. My light is all broke in and shines better'n yours. But you're a good kid, so I wouldn't mind switchin' with ya."

I wouldn't mind switching either, since mine was stolen from a place just a few houses down the street, and if anyone saw it they would figure Duke broke in the house instead of me and Posey, so I switched.

When I got home that afternoon, it was obvious something was going on. Nancy was on the phone telling my mother she had to come home. Diane had fainted downtown in front of the bank. Everyone thought she was at work at the bus terminal luncheonette. Turns out she had quit that job.

It was determined that she had "fainted from the heat," but Mom must have figured something was up, and she got Diane a job at Jay's. She also began taking me to work with them every day I didn't go to school. It wasn't bad. I got to hang out in the freezer and eat all the Jay's frozen dessert I wanted.

Chapter Ten
Loaves and Fishing
March

Fishing had become a big thing by March, and Duke promised to take us night fishing with him. My mother complained, but I whined until she said okay. This didn't always work. I think she was getting tired of the whole situation.

We not only went fishing in the dark, but we went fishing in the dark on top of the dam, over a river, or a canal. Whatever it was, we couldn't see it in the totally moonless night. Duke shined his light on the dam from the path that we took from the car. The top of the structure where we stood was only about three or four feet wide, and I was more than a little concerned when Duke said,

"Y'all go out in the middle there and fish. It's where the big ones are." I noticed he wasn't going to come with us, which meant we didn't have a light. Posey went first, then Garrett. I held back since I couldn't even see the dam, but eventually I crawled out into the dark. The three of us went on hands and knees, dragging our fishing poles, the twenty or so yards out to what we felt must be the middle of the concrete wall. On the right side of us was water. I could hear it splashing against the wall only a few feet from the top. On the other side there was no sound at all, so I figured the water was quite a ways down. When I bumped into Garrett's butt, I realized they had stopped.

"I can't see anything," Garrett said. "Can you?"

"Nope," I answered. "Posey, can you see anything?"

Posey didn't answer right away. Then after a few seconds he said, "Turn around and go back."

Now I was leading the way into the darkness on all fours. I made up a prayer that could have been the same one Moses uttered. "God, I don't know where the hell we are or where I'm going, but could You help me get there?" The only reason I knew I was safe was when the ground beneath my hands and knees turned from the cold of the concrete into the warmth of the dirt.

The three of us regrouped, standing up on the bank of the canal or river. I wasn't even sure which it was, and I couldn't have cared less.

Then a light came along the bank. It was Duke, proudly lighting the way with my stolen flashlight.

"Y'all must be as dumb as the ass end of a hoss. You fall off that dam and you'd probly git killed." Duke laughed. Then he shone the light at the dam. One wrong move and we would have fallen into the deep water or over the other edge, down thirty or so feet to a trickle of water and stones at the bottom.

At that moment, I realized that Posey and Garrett's daddy was out of his mind.

I blessed myself for God having saved me, and I walked silently to the truck. The other two followed me.

"No more fishin'?" Duke asked.

"Nope," I said.

"Why not, L'il Boston? You afraid?"

"Fish don't cost that much at the store," I said, and the three of us boys laughed.

Within half an hour we were back at our places, and I went to bed and prayed, thanking God again for not killing me while I was in a state of sin. Before I went to sleep, I said a silent Act of Contrition.

A few days later, all us kids were playing on the other side of our small ditch in the patch of desert when suddenly Duke stood in the driveway.

"C'mon. We're going to the store. I gotta buy some bread. Y'all can ride in the back of the truck."

Being stupid children, we scrambled into the back of the pickup.

Duke drove right past Safeway and kept going. About fifteen minutes later, he stopped at a main irrigation ditch. The ditch was very wide, and very deep, and was made, bottom and sides, out of cement. It had a dirt road running along the side of it. Duke came to the back of the truck and pulled out a coil of heavy rope.

He tied one end to the trailer hitch on the truck and tied a loop in the other end. He told Posey to hold on to the loop end, and then picked him up by the scruff of his shirt and the back of his belt and threw him into the water, rope and all. He then jumped into the truck and drove along the edge of the ditch, skimming Posey along the top of the water in the canal. I thought, *That can't be safe.*

Next, it was Garrett's turn. He slid along the top of the water for a while and then couldn't hold on any longer and skittered to a stop. Duke backed up and Posey threw the rope to his brother, who held onto it until he was close enough to the edge to climb out. "Yup," I thought. "Out of his mind."

"Your turn, L'il Boston," Duke shouted from the cab

of the truck.

'No, it's not," I answered.

"Why not?" he called. "You ascared?"

"I can't swim," I said.

Posey turned to me. His eyes were wide like the time we turned over a rock in the desert and a diamondback came out.

"Run," he said. "He's going to throw you in."

I ran. And quickly Duke gave up. "I'm jes gonna show you how to swim," he called to me.

"No you aren't," I answered. I didn't believe him, so I ran for a while, and then I walked home. It took a long time, but I figured it was better than being dead.

When I reached home, I was so tired I went directly to my room and tucked myself under the bed spread. I fell asleep almost immediately.

In my repeating nightmare, I was in a box that was strangely called The Britannica, bobbing across an unending ocean on my way to China. It was just as the nuns had told us. I had done something wrong and had been put in a large wooden box she had called the Britannica, and I was headed for China, never to see my mother and father again. Then, just as quickly, I was being dragged up the sidewalk on Winter Street in Milford, Massachusetts toward St Mary's Church. The nun had the face of my Aunt Kathleen, and in one hand she held the hand basket to hell. I was pushed inside the church doors and shoved down the center aisle to the first pew. It was frightening. The priest with the purple robes was chanting the names of saints and calling for Jesus to help him expel a demon. The nun prayed and held me in the pew while she shouted in my face.

From that day in the first grade when I had been put through my attempted exorcism by a visiting priest and God's bouncer-nun all because I had punched one of their favorite students, I had had this recurring dream. I woke sweating cold under the blanket.

The next weekend, something terrible happened to Posey and Garrett's family.

Their cousin drowned in the canal while learning how to swim. No one said how it might have happened. But again, I thanked God for making me smart enough to know Duke was an asshole.

I didn't tell anyone what had happened to me. I didn't tell anyone about my suspicions that someone might have thrown that kid into the canal, since I now knew that some people thought that was a way to teach someone to swim.

It wasn't a long time later that Duke made himself a

new frog gig and gave me his old one. It wasn't the kind with the nail on the end. It was the kind with the claw device that closed on the frog when you gigged him. Dad thought that was "very nice of Duke." I agreed.

He tried to give me back my flashlight, but I told him, "No sir, Mr. Duke. A deal's a deal."

By the end of March, I had learned from Posey how to make a weapon by cutting a piece of bamboo a couple feet long and an inch or so in diameter, then making a slice on one end, from front to back, at a diagonal about two inches long so we could fit a rock snuggly in the slice. When you whipped it, the rock went twice as far as you could throw it, and twice as fast. I had no idea why we were making weapons, but it killed the better part of a hot afternoon, so I just went along and made what Posey called our "cowboy slingshots."

Posey also taught me to smoke tumbleweed. He said it could make me see stuff that wasn't there. We would stop a tumbleweed, which was just a very dried out ball of vegetation. We would break off a piece about as long as a cigarette, light one end, and smoke it just like a Pall Mall. I smoked it, but it didn't seem to work like Posey said it would. It was like smoking a really old cigarette. I found out later that he must have been talking about Jimson weed.

Chapter Eleven
Unfazed by Fortitude
April

At the beginning of April, I found out why we were making weapons.

It was on the same day Posey and I discovered three cardboard boxes of discarded artists' paint in the field near the auto junkyard. Inside each box were dozens of dark blue, torpedo-like plastic tubes of hardened paint about six or seven inches long and a couple of inches in diameter. They resembled torpedoes with a nipple on the front. When they were new, an artist could cut the nipple off the front and squeeze out the paint, but in this old and hardened state, they made great missiles.

Behind our houses in a field beyond the junk yard,

there was a large flat rock. We had all ditched Crazy Willie again, which we were doing more often now, because most of the time he lived up to his name. We were playing in the field when suddenly there were five or six other kids on bicycles in the field with us.

We walked over to meet them.

"This is our turf," the big one said.

"What does that mean?" I asked.

"You aren't allowed here."

I was all for talking to them, but Posey had a different idea.

"We're allowed anywhere we want to go," he said and stepped forward.

A quick count told me we were out-numbered, and although Posey wanted to settle things right then, I thought maybe we could use a little planning.

"We'll meet you here this afternoon," I said. "Whoever wins the fight can play in the field. Whoever loses can't."

I didn't know it, but we were about to have our first gang fight, and we were all under twelve years old.

In the time between the first encounter and the second, we planned. I told Posey, "We can use these paint things like artillery." I had the best arm, so I volunteered to be the long-range barrage. "The rest of you get up in their faces and fire rocks and stuff at them, and while you're keeping them busy, I'll pick 'em off one at a time."

It sounded like a good idea, and I was satisfied with staying out of their range. When it came time, Posey, Garrett, Tim, and Danny Boy set up our front line with pockets full of rocks. I stayed back, and I found out that my little brother Dennis was not dumb. As the fight started, Dennis stood right beside me and started firing paint missiles from the box.

"I figure you can use some help," he said and smiled, fully knowing what I had done. The two of us lobbed the paint rockets in on our opponents while the others kept them busy by firing rocks from ten feet apart with the bamboo sling shots we had made. Between Dennis and me, we hit every one of them at least once, and when they started watching what we were doing with our "artillery," our front line pummeled them. They started backing up and continued until they were off the field and the playground was ours. We celebrated. We never saw them again, and no one ever figured out that Dennis and I had stayed out of range the whole time, safely lobbing in paint rockets and laughing.

The next day, however, became a turning point in our group. I was walking behind the row of apartments when the back door to Crazy Willie's house opened up. I heard his father's voice. "Kick his Yankee butt," he shouted, and

Willie stood holding open the screen door reluctantly.

"Get him," his old man shouted and pushed him out the back door.

The first thing I noticed was Willie had one of those serrated-edge steak knives in his hand.

"It was your plan," he shouted, "and you didn't get punished." I guessed he had squealed after all.

"Don't be stupid," I said.

Willie kept coming, and when he was close enough I stepped in and grabbed his arm near the wrist, ducked under it and stepped behind him while still holding his wrist. I pushed his arm up his back. "Willie, I will break your arm if you don't drop the knife." I pushed harder, and he wriggled, trying to get free. He was nearly free, but he didn't know it, so he dropped the knife. I picked it up and threw it into the junkyard where the dog lived.

Willie turned and ran into his house. Stunned, I continued on around the end of the apartment building and started toward my own place. As I passed the front door of Willie's house, he was being pushed back outside by his old man. At least this time he didn't have a knife.

We fought for a while. He would swing and miss, and I would hit him in the stomach. It went on for a while until a crowd had formed, and Nancy shouted, "Oh, for God's sake Johnny, hit him in the face."

So I did, and he ran into the house crying. His old man beat him up for losing, and I went home. I was confused, but so much since I arrived here in the desert had confused me that this was just another thing to put up with. It didn't bother me much. I wasn't even mad at Willie. He was only doing what his idiot father told him to do. And we were supposed to do that, right? Honor thy mother and father?

That afternoon, I went outside, and Garrett was waiting for me. He too seemed to have some reason for wanting a fight.

"My Daddy says you have to get your ass kicked," he said.

"I'm not going to fight you, Garrett. You're my friend. And your daddy is out of his mind."

"I don't care. My daddy said I have to fight you, or I could beat your sister. I can't fight no girl."

"Well, you can't fight Nancy and win," I said with a laugh. "I don't care what your daddy says. You're my friend, and I'm not going to fight you, and if you fight with Nancy, she'll just beat you like she did Posey."

He attacked me. I grabbed him in a headlock and pulled him to the ground. Posey started out of his house, but his mother, who had heard the whole thing, grabbed him at the door and said, "Nope, he deserves it."

Again, I told Garrett that I didn't want to fight him. I held him tight around his neck for a few more minutes, and when he realized I wasn't going to fight or let go, he said, "Okay, let me up."

I did, and he walked into his house.

Life on South Second Street was getting pretty lonely, but baseball had become important and took my mind off the problems in the neighborhood. I had gotten the call. I had made the team again, so had Willie. We were actually on the same team. I pitched, and he played second base.

We played three times a week, which kept us from getting into trouble, but the others in the line of apartments had no outlet and were planning stuff to keep them occupied. Posey had forced his younger brother to make up with me, and when I wasn't playing ball, we hung out together again.

Then came the word I didn't understand.

"You know that Mormon girl who lives down south of here?" Posey asked one afternoon while we were forcing scorpions into coke bottles with a stick to sell as good luck charms, not realizing that the good luck was that the scorpions hadn't killed us.

I nodded. She was a good kid, kind of cute, dark hair, about our age. She lived down by the orange groves.

"We're going to rape her. Want to come?"

I hesitated, and Posey added, "If ya got the guts."

"Sure," I said. I had no idea what rape meant, but we had just made up from the fights, and I wanted to be part of the group of friends again.

"We're going to do it this Saturday," Posey said. "We'll meet at the end of the ditch near the street, and when her mother goes shopping, she'll be alone in the house. We'll do it then."

"Okay," I said.

For some reason, I knew this was probably something I didn't want to do without finding what it was, so I asked Diane.

She pinned me with a stare and wrinkled her brow. "Do you know what rape means?" she asked.

"No, not really. What does it mean?" I asked.

"It doesn't really matter, except that you're not going."

"What does it mean?"

"It means force her to have sex with you. Do you even know what that is? Sex?"

I sort of did, thanks to Cindy, but I said no to cut the conversation short.

"I'll take care of this," Diane said. "Don't talk to them about it. Just don't go with them. Okay?"

I agreed. My older sister, who had been my mother for

a month or so, was formidable. She was sixteen years old now and was, on her own, going to stop a rape. I don't know what she did, but she walked off to Posey's house. She knocked on the door, and the mother let her in, and the whole thing didn't happen.

Not only that, but Posey and Garrett never said another word about it to me. It was as if the whole plan had never been made, had never even been talked about. No one's mother got outwardly involved, no one's father. And the brothers never spoke of it again. Diane simply walked off into the heat of a Phoenix afternoon, stepped inside their front door, and the whole thing stopped.

"Thank God."

Or Diane.

I was finally going to see Indians.

It was late May, and we were going to play the team from Mesa. I liked my baseball coach, but he was a better coach than he was a person. He sat us down in a circle on the infield between first base and the mound, and he sat down next to me. He told us about the upcoming game.

"This team from Mesa is mostly Indians," he said. "They're from Mesa and Apache Junction." He looked around the circle. "They are very good. Just like us, they haven't been beaten yet, and they are winning by scoring a ton of runs." He smiled at me.

"But they haven't met John yet." He patted me on the shoulder. "If they don't score a lot of runs, we can beat them. Their pitching isn't as good as ours. Get a good night's sleep, eat a good lunch, and show up ready to play. No one wants to lose to Indians, right?" He made a motion as if he was scalping himself.

I said good-bye to him as we reached the snow cone machine in left field just beyond the fence.

"Make sure you're ready for this one," he said. "We're counting on you."

I nodded, bought a cherry snow cone, looked both ways, bolted across the street, and headed home.

We played Friday games under the lights because it was cooler, and a lot of people showed up to watch. The stands were full along both baselines. I liked pitching at night because it made my fastball harder to see, since some of our lights were out.

We took the field first. I felt good. During warm-ups the ball went wherever I wanted it to go.

In the first inning, I struck out the side. Three up, three down. As I left the mound, I saw a strange thing. The Mesa coach smiled and tipped his hat to me.

We got a run in our half of the inning, and then we took the field again.

The first batter bunted. I thought, "Damn, he's fast," as

he pulled up safe at first base.

The next five batters bunted. I was not as good a fielder as I was a pitcher, and before I knew it the game was tied and there were two outs. They had runners on first and third. A bloop single over Willie's head brought in two more runs.

Coach came to the mound.

"Throw curves," he said, and walked back to the bench.

The next batter struck out, and we were out of the inning but it was 3-1.

We got a run back, and when the first batter in the next inning bunted, I overthrew first. As I watched him trot into second base, I knew what I had to do.

Coach came out again and said, "Calm down and throw strikes. You can field better than this. One play at a time."

As I said, I knew what to do.

I bounced the next fastball off the batter's neck. As he trotted to first base crying, I glared at him and said, "Bunt that!" I turned and tipped my hat to the Mesa coach. I know I was supposed to make believe it was a mistake, but I didn't feel like it.

After that, most of the rest of the team seemed to take three swings and hustle back to the safety of their bench.

But we lost 4-3.

The high school coach spoke after the game with my mother and father and my coach. They laughed a lot, slapped each other on the back, and we all went home. I was satisfied that I had put the fear of the Lord into that team that we would have to play two more times during the year.

I was about to find out about a beatitude I hadn't learned at St. Mary's school; the one that says, *Blessed are the nice children, because what goes around comes around.*

South Mountain loomed over the city from about 2,500 feet up. When there were clouds, they chopped off the top of the mountain. I had wanted to visit it ever since I had been told about the Lost Dutchman's Mine. Today, we were invited to take a trip with Duke to see the lookout point. We were to take the road all the way up to the summit. It turned out I had been lied to. The Dutchman's mine was actually in the Superstition Mountains out by Apache Junction, east of Phoenix, not south.

Duke and my mother and father were in the front seat with Neil. And there were eight kids, my whole family, Posey, Garrett and DeDe, in the open pickup bed. We should have known something was wrong when Mrs. Duke didn't want to come.

The climb up the mountain was beautiful. With each cutback, more of the city appeared below us, the buildings getting smaller and smaller in the distance. In the center of the city, the buildings were taller than the rest, and soon we could see the entire city below us. The biggest buildings seemed to be about two inches tall.

At the top of the mountain sat a small stone building. We walked down to the edge and looked out the side that faced the city far below us. After a short time, my mother called, and we all rumbled back into the pickup truck for the ride home.

We rolled out onto the road that clung to the side of the mountain. Duke seemed intent on giving us a really good ride by taking the corners at about twice the speed limit. In the back, we rolled from one side to the other, bumping into each other. I kept trying to control myself, and when I couldn't, it stopped being fun. Garrett bumped his head and got cut. Posey's eyes were wide. "He never goes this fast," he said. The girls all held onto each other in fright. Almost immediately, the truck slammed to a stop. My father got out and walked to where we sat. I could tell he was angry. "Hold on tight," he said. "Do not let go!"

He returned to the cab and stepped in.

The truck lurched and careened down the mountain

at the edge of out of control while we held on, our feet flinging back and forth. The tires squealed when we turned, and we could feel the ass end of the truck sliding. All we could see was the side where the mountain rose up, but we knew for certain the drop to the city below on the other side would kill us if we went over. I pulled myself up so I could see over the side. We were so close to the edge of the road that all I could see was the straight-down side of a cliff. We were only feet from the edge. I laid down, trying to flatten myself against the floor of the truck bed, and my mind clung to the side of the mountain, hoping to keep the truck from going over. I counted every breath and prayed to God that my family wouldn't die here on the side of a Phoenix mountain. This time God said okay. When we reached the bottom, Duke stopped and pulled over. The adults were shouting at each other, and since the windows were open, we could hear every word they said.

"Are you insane?" my mother shouted.

"I just wanted to put you in your husband's arms," Duke answered. "Wasn't it fun? You weren't ascared, were you Boston?"

My father sat quiet in total anger for a few seconds and then said, "You are fecking insane. What if you blew a tire? We'd all be dead, you goddamn fool."

Duke shook his head and put the truck in gear."I think the brakes were going," he said, but no one believed him.

My knees had turned to Jell-o, my stomach fought to not lose everything I had eaten in days, my eyes watered, and my hands sweated. Even sitting on the surface roads at the bottom of the mountain, I felt as if at any moment I might fall off the edge of the world. I held onto the side of the truck bed and squeezed until my knuckles turned white.

When the truck began rolling again, I crawled into the right front corner of the truck bed, and I made myself as small as humanly possible for the ride back to South Second Street.

Now, I knew what the fear of the Lord felt like.

I realized how the batter must have felt when he saw that baseball coming straight at his head.

I went to my bed and climbed under the covers. This time when I fell asleep, there was a new addition to the nightmare.

I stood at the altar, being held firmly by the scruff of my neck by a nun. She dangled me over the side of a mountain and screamed at me to "leave the boy alone!" She searched deep through my eyes, directly into my soul, and told me she'd had enough of me. She conspired with a priest who didn't speak English to rid me of my inclinations toward evil. I kicked, pushed, and ran along the edge of the road with the mountain on one side and the fall to my death on the other. Then, at the moment I felt fright would overtake my sanity, I reached the bottom with the brown grass and the level base path, and I walked to first base, shaking. A face in the mountain looked at me and said, "Bunt that!"

I woke up and went into the living room. My mother sat watching TV.

"I shouldn't have thrown at that kid's head," I said to her.

"No, you shouldn't have," she said, "but that's what you were told to do. It's what you do with batters who bunt, isn't it? High and inside?"

I thought about how often I had been told that by my father, who had always been my coach until now.

"But you are right," she continued. "You shouldn't have thrown at his head." She paused, then added, "Quite a ride, wasn't it?"

"I was scared," I said, and walked to the couch to sit next to her.

"Me too," she said. She put her arm around me, and we watched TV until our insides stopped shaking.

Baseball had always been my second religion and my

second family, and now I threw myself into the game, since the other two had been kind of messed up. In practice, we learned how to field bunts, and they never became a problem again. Our team was sailing along in first place, and I was pitching every other game when baseball presented another lesson and taught me one more thing about right and wrong.

It was my turn to pitch again, but I had left the house late, and the coach had told Willie if I didn't show up, he would be the one who had to pitch. When I crossed the last irrigation ditch and walked toward the two teams getting ready, it was almost time for the game to start. Willie was already warming up when Dave, our catcher, stood and held a hand up, telling Willie to stop throwing. We really wanted to remain in first place, so when they realized I was going to make it to the game, my team applauded. I could see Willie's shoulders drop. It probably was at least one of the reasons for what happened later in the game.

The team we were playing was from Chandler, and they were pretty good too. We were up, but not by much, and a ball was hit to Willie. He was a good fielder and usually made this play, but today he missed the ball. After the ball was thrown in from the outfield, and the guy was safe on first base, Drake, our shortstop, and the coach's son, shouted at Willie, "Stop the damn ball, moron!"

It happened quickly. Willie dropped his glove and charged at Drake. Most of us laughed as they flurried into a ball of dust just behind second base. One person was not amused. Drake's father stormed out onto the field. He went right for Crazy Willie.

As he passed the mound, I made a decision.

"Your son started it," I said. He stopped for a second, glared at me, and said, "If I want your opinion, I'll ask for it." He continued on to where the two combatants were.

"Apologize!" he shouted at Willie.

"That's just not fair," I said to myself. I took off my hat and team shirt, folded the shirt nicely and placed it on the mound. I meticulously placed my hat on top of it. Then I strode off the mound and went and sat in the bleachers. The fans were stunned, and I got a little embarrassed because they were all looking at me, and I was half naked.

When the coach turned around, the first thing he saw was the empty mound, then the shirt and hat. He searched the edges of the field, first at the bench, and then he saw me in the stands. He walked straight to the fence behind home plate and said, "Get on the field."

"No," I said.

"Get on the damn field."

"No. I told you your kid started it, and you made Willie apologize. I ain't playing for you. You can have the shirt and hat though." I smiled.

We walked home, me, Dennis, my mother and father, and Neil. We three boys kept laughing and passing looks back and forth. My mother and father were totally silent.

When we got to the house, I said, "I'm going to go get an orange."

"No, you're not," my mother said. "Come in here."

Mum and Dad sat at the kitchen table, and she pointed to an empty chair for me.

When I was seated, Dad said, "So, what was that all about?"

I thought for what seemed to be an eternity. Then I said, "What?"

It was a Mexican standoff.

Everyone stared at each other.

Mum broke the silence. "Do you know you just quit your team?"

"Yup."

Dad added, "Are you sure you want to do that?"

"Yup."

"How come?" Mum asked.

"I'm tired of it."

"Of what?" she asked.

"Everything. Nothing is fair here. Rich people have lawns and cars and orange trees, and we have nothing. We have a damn ditch and scorpions. Did you notice our lights in right field are mostly out? I bet Enchanto Park has lights. Coach just wanted to jump Willie because of where we come from."

"Didn't Willie try to knife you?" Dad asked.

I nodded.

"So why did you care if he got in trouble?"

"I don't know. I guess Willie's us, and they're them."

Mum stood up from the table. "We're getting out of here," she said and put her arm around me. "My God, what were we thinking?"

It suddenly made so much sense to me. This wasn't the kid I'd been before I got here: stealing, lying, knife fights, death rides, rape, gang fights, and now this. My mother was right. We had to get out of here, or this is who I would remain being and how I would keep acting. At that point, she had to decide who was "us" and who was "them."

A few days later, I told Posey. "We're moving. I think we're going up by Camelback."

"That's where the rich people live," he said.

"Is it?"

"Yes, you'll be one of those bastards who make up

names for us. They call us pachuco. You'll be one of them."

"I'm just going to be myself," I said. "And, by the way, I don't think they call us pachuco. I think it's only kids like Freddie and Ross. I think they call us white trash."

"No," Posey insisted. "Y'all gonna be one of them. With the lawns and fancy cars. You're gonna hate us, jes like they do. My daddy was right. Y'all think you're better'n us cuz y'all come from Boston."

"That's just nuts. Your daddy is nuts, and I've never even been to Boston. I've hardly been out of Milford and here," I said, and stood up to leave. Until now, the two of us had been friends from the beginning, but now I saw a change. He was stuck here in South Phoenix in the barrio and going to Rio Vista school. He had few friends, and now his best friend was moving north to the relative affluence three jobs could buy; my father's, my mother's, and Diane's.

Within a week, my mother told me to go to the market and get some boxes so we could pack for the move.

I was walking home from the market with four cardboard boxes when I was confronted by Garrett, Posey and Willie. They blocked my way as I passed behind the stone foundation of a burned-out house. I couldn't walk around them. There wasn't enough room. My apartment was only twenty yards away, and my mother was inside waiting for these boxes to finish her packing, but first I was going to have to deal with these three. Two of them I had already beaten once, but one at a time, and I was pretty certain that I couldn't take Posey one on one, never mind three on one. I was planning to throw the boxes at them when they were close enough and try to run by them and beat them to my house.

Then, I noticed Nancy stepping out the back door. Sheila had seen what was happening and told my mother, who immediately turned to Nancy and said, "Go help your brother."

My sister began walking purposefully toward us. The three didn't notice her coming from behind.

"You think you're better'n us," Garrett said. He spit on the ground in front of him.

"No, I don't," I said.

"I think he's right," Posey said. I had seen that face before. Just before Posey did something stupid, he had always looked just like his daddy.

"You're gonna get a ass whoopin,' Yankee," Willie said, finally convinced that with this help he could win. I couldn't help thinking, this was the boy I had just stuck up for by quitting baseball.

Nancy picked up a four-foot-long piece of a two-by-four that lay against the fence to the junk yard. As she got within striking distance, she swung it hard into Posey's legs. He grabbed one leg that seemed to be hurt more than the other and screamed in pain. Nancy swung it at Garrett who backed up, and Willie just ran like hell.

She motioned for me to walk over to her, and when I got there, she said, "Come on, let's go home."

I started to turn back to see if anyone followed us, and she said, "Don't even look back. They aren't coming."

Two days later, we moved.

As the taxi pulled away from South Second Street, Posey and Garrett stood in the field. They waved goodbye. I never saw them again.

Chapter Thirteen
Home Counsel
June

The new house had some things that were different, but, sadly, some that weren't.

It had three bedrooms that each opened up onto a single patio where plants my mother called "succulents" grew. There were lizards the size of California chili peppers and horned toads as big as baseballs. We even had a fenced-in backyard. It wasn't big, but it was only ours. Later, I found out why.

The first few weeks we spent with what seemed to be Mum's new obsession. She wanted to play whist. From morning to bed time, we played cards, or we watched TV. We were weeks into our new living quarters, and I had no idea what was outside our yard.

We had found a pogo stick in the back room, and Dennis and I and Nancy learned to use it in the driveway. One afternoon Neil picked it up, and we all stared at each other in surprise. Until now he hadn't tried it, and we were all a bit worried when he picked it up. He was only seven. He jumped up on it and hopped off down the driveway, turned without getting off, and hopped back to where we were all standing. He jumped off it and smiled up at us.

We found a mandolin, and, with Mum's enthusiastic insistence, we began trying to play it, but always there was whist, pitch, and TV.

One morning, I edged toward the end of the walkway with the intention of taking a walk in my new environment, but as I took a left onto the sidewalk, Mum called from the window.

"Where do you think you're going?" she called.

"Just taking a walk," I said.

"No, you're not."

"You mean I can't leave the yard?"

"Diane is going out later. You can go with her."

After the past ten months of freedom, I couldn't believe I was to be locked into the yard unless I had one of my sisters walk with me.

I spent about a half-hour throwing rocks at pigeons, then Diane came out the front door. "Let's go," she said and smiled.

It was dusk as we walked the streets that my friends in South Phoenix called "where the rich people lived, with lawns and fancy cars." There were lawns and driveways and even some fancy cars, but there was something about the new place that made me feel uneasy.

Maybe my uneasiness stemmed from the fact that I had just moved from a place where I fit in, and now lived where we didn't. Not fitting in, I decided, could be dangerous. At least that's what my mother seemed to think.

We had walked about a mile when Diane said, "There it is."

Suddenly, I realized we were just going to a market. Bread, milk, Kool-Aid, and a pack of Pall Malls later, we started out of the store. It had turned to dusk, and the street lights had come on. The manager of the store came out right behind us. "Miss," he said, and he took Diane gently by the arm.

"You can't walk around out here like that."

I saw nothing that would explain his "like that" statement.

She was wearing her shorts and a t-shirt that she had

worn several times since we had arrived in Phoenix. I thought she looked nice.

"I'm sorry," he said, and he did seem truly sorry, "but you can't be out here on the streets in the dark like this."

"We live just down the street," she said.

"I'll get someone." He turned and quickly stepped back inside. He called to a boy who had been stocking a shelf with liquor bottles. As the boy began walking to where we were, the manager came back outside and turned to Diane again. "You won't need to worry. He's a good boy. He'll take you right home."

We followed the boy out to a pickup truck in the parking lot, and he drove us home, trying not to keep his eyes on Diane too long. He even made believe he was interested in who I was.

"So," he said to me, leaning forward past Diane. "What's your name?" His tone told me he was only using me to get to Diane, and I didn't like him talking down to me. I figured he didn't much care what my name was at all.

"The Great Garloo," I answered, and watched out the window at the neon lights that lined the street.

"Oh, okay," he said and sat up.

When we got to our house, he said nervously to Diane, "Do you think I could call you?"

Diane took the price marker from his shirt pocket and wrote something on his hand. "Don't lose that," she said, and we slid across the front seat and out of the truck.

She was interested in the boy she had just met, and I was worried that the manager felt we shouldn't walk around on the streets at night. I always had felt safer when we lived in the barrio.

We ate better now. My mother brought home five-gallon containers of Jay's frozen dessert, and Dad brought home all the nectarines, peaches, and bananas that were a couple of days old.

The first day he walked in with brown paper grocery bags full of fruit, I smiled at him.

"Water damage?" I asked, and he laughed.

Since it was all free, we got to eat as much as we wanted, as often as we wanted, but we weren't allowed to leave the yard alone. It seemed we were to be more careful of these people who all looked like us than we had been of the Mexican people we had lived with for almost a year.

One hot afternoon, Diane took me with her to a park not far from the house. There was a wading pool in the middle with benches all around it. The water was only about two feet deep. Both the pool and the park were totally empty. In South Phoenix the pool would have been crawling with kids, but here the refrigerated houses were more comfortable inside than out.

The concrete the pool was made of was smooth and comfortable. The water was cool enough, and there was a fountain in the middle that shot water about three or four feet high into the air. I sat under it.

I could see out of the mist umbrella it created into the green park. The sunlight through the mist made a rainbow all around me. I could see the fruit trees, and Camelback Mountain looming purple in the distance. The sky was a perfect blue, as it was during every day that wasn't part of the monsoon season. A teenage boy with a white shirt and blue jeans had entered the park on the other side with a large brown dog. They were playing catch with a tennis ball. It was a beautifully perfect day. The boy threw the ball, and it bounced until it reached the wading pool. The dog raced to pick it up, and, just before retrieving the ball, the dog stopped to urinate in the pool. I immediately got out, and Diane and I laughed, but it wasn't funny.

The dog had destroyed a beautiful day. It hadn't been the first time our lives had been comfortable and then had suddenly been torn apart through no fault of our own. We were getting used to it.

Diane and I sat on the bench and watched the dog return the ball to his master. We didn't talk until she said, "I guess sometimes you just have to call it quits. I really want to go home."

I agreed, and we walked out of the park and back to the house.

Mum waited for us with a smile.

"We just got a phone call," she said. "They want you to be on the Phoenix All-Star team."

That didn't make any sense to me. "But I quit my team," I said.

"They don't seem to care. Your first game is Saturday. You'll be playing Tucson. You're pitching."

That night, my nightmare came again. It had become clearer now, and I felt in my sleep the same fright I had felt on the day it had actually happened.

Mulchahey had just pushed in front of me in line back home while I was talking to my friend Elaine. I pushed him against the side of the granite school building, and he was rescued by Sister Mary Patrick. She pushed and pulled me up the street to the church, where she and a visiting priest had tried to exorcise a demon out of me who wasn't there. I had been so frightened then that I was still dreaming of that day now. Now, however, other things had entered the dream, like the reckless charge down the cutbacks of South Mountain's summit road, the dam I crawled across in the dark, and the death of Posey's cousin. Now added to it was this dog pissing in my swimming pool.

I woke up sweating and shaking. I pulled the bedspread over my head and waited for morning.

Chapter Fourteen
Understanding My Unimportance
July

When I joined the All-Star team at Enchanto Park, the two coaches walked out to meet us in the parking lot where our new neighbor had dropped us off. It appeared they had been waiting to see if I would show up. For a short time, I felt important.

My mother and father met them.

"You know he quit his team, don't you?" my father said to one of them as I arrived.

"Don't care," the smaller coach said. The other added, "He had spent the whole season with that coach except a few games. He's eligible. It's legal."

He handed me a team shirt and hat, and I started

putting them on.

I expected to find Willie, but didn't. "Is Willie here?"

They didn't answer, but I saw that he wasn't.

"You all set?" the big coach asked me.

The smaller one chimed in, "We're playing Tucson. I guess you know that if we win this, we'll all be going to the TV game."

"TV game?" I asked.

"The Little League World Series," the little guy said. "How's that sinker of yours working?"

"I don't know," I said. "I haven't pitched since I quit my team."

The adults decided not to deal with what I had said. When I got to the bench, I saw that Dave, our catcher, had made the team too.

"Anyone else make it?" I asked him.

"Just you and me," he said.

As I took the mound, I wasn't sure how I felt about the field being surrounded by so many fans.

During warm-ups, I saw their whole team standing along the third baseline and watching me.

"Play ball!"

By the fourth inning, we were up 1-0. It was hot.

I was having a good day. My father had taught me to hold the baseball along the seams. It was how I had always pitched. It gave me a natural sinking fastball, and the big hitters on the Tucson team were all trying to hit the home runs they were used to hitting. In the fifth inning, I felt as if it was impossible for them to hit the ball at all.

Then it happened.

Just after the first pitch of the fifth inning, I began having a difficult time finding enough air to breathe. I stepped off the mound and removed my hat. It seemed that while the hat was off, I could breathe. I took a deep breath and put the hat back on, stepped onto the mound, and threw a pitch. Strike two.

Again, I stepped off the mound. We were still up 1-0. All I had to do was get through six more outs, and I would be taking this team and the two coaches to "the TV game."

I took off my hat, and the field blurred.

"Time out!" the big coach called and ran to the mound. "Are you okay?" he asked.

"There is just no air under my hat," I heard myself say.

It was the last thing I heard until I was being revived while lying on the bench in the dugout.

"What happened?" I asked my mother, who was standing over me.

"You passed out," she said.

The field was empty. My team was all walking away from the field.

"Did we win?"

"No," my father said. "You lost, 2-1."

"You pitched great, kid," the little coach said, and he walked off without even asking how I was feeling.

I realized I had been lying on the bench. Both coaches had left me lying there passed out until the game was over. They had never even told my parents I was still unconscious until the game had ended. It was obvious to me that they couldn't have cared less about me except that I could pitch. I was happy they didn't make it to the TV game.

I sat up on the bench and found my parents sitting next to me. They hadn't known the truth of what had happened. They thought I had been revived and was sitting in the dugout watching the game.

"Did you just wake up?" my father asked.

"A few minutes ago," I said.

"Did you see the last innings of the game?"

"No."

"Hey!" he shouted after the coaches, and he walked off to catch up with them

My mother put her hand on my shoulder. "Let's get out of here," she said, and we walked off back to the parking lot where our new neighbor had parked the car. I found out later that the temperature was well over 100 degrees, and it was hotter on the mound.

Chapter Fifteen
Sacraments Revisited
August

It was decided that Diane, Neil, and I would go home with my mother. My father, Dennis, and the twins would stay behind. Dad had begged an advance on his paycheck again for enough money to send us home. The plan was for him to stay behind with half his family in order to pay it off and save enough so the rest of them could follow us.

I was going home. I was tired. I couldn't stop sleeping during the bus ride. I figured I was doing what Diane called, "getting depressed." I searched out the bus window hoping for a reunion with my other self who had followed us when we had journeyed to Arizona only a year ago. My God, I thought, was it only a year? Am I only eleven?

As the bus rolled out of the desert and into the mountains of New Mexico, I leaned against the window so the air conditioning that blew up from the bottom of the glass could cool my face. In the blur of the scenery flying by, I saw my last year flash through my head.

A year ago, I was a kid who had a home, a family, and a relationship with God.

I thought back over the past months, remembering the pain of my toothache, punching a grown man in the face and breaking his nose. I pictured my father telling me to not trust a priest, but instead I should trust a bartender. There were threatened knife fights that might have killed my father and left us alone in a barrio, and real knife fights that could have left me cut up or dead. There were visions of Ned butchering a cow as a means of sustenance and a source of entertainment. I searched the faces on the bus and found I knew no one other than my family. Turning my attention back out the window, I wondered when I had started stealing what I wanted, even from a church. My father had threatened the life of a young man for something that probably wasn't his fault, and I had set a bull running after a bunch of kids. He could have killed them, but, at the time, it seemed right.

There had been sex thanks to Cindy, and nearly a rape, playing with knives, almost drowning, and us kids being used for the entertainment of adults. I remembered being hungry, being afraid, being bullied, bullying other kids, breaking and entering a neighbor's home, a gang fight, and friends turning on each other. And there was, of course, the chill of horror when you feel that at any moment you might plummet over the side of a mountain and die.

I turned to my mother and nudged her. She turned toward me.

"Was it really just a year?" I asked.

She nodded and returned to the window and whatever was over the side of a mountain road. I almost thought I was dreaming, when a little red sports car flew by the bus. Mum and I watched as the car pulled ahead of us, then on a turn he took too fast he swerved and ended up off the highway in a ditch.

"Did you see that?" I asked.

"I did," she said, and we went back to day dreaming.

I fell asleep, and when I woke up, the bus was being pulled over by a police cruiser. The cop came up to the door of the bus and climbed up the steps. He told the bus driver that a guy in a sports car had turned him in, said the bus had forced him off the road.

"Well, that's just not true," my mother said, and both men looked at her.

"Did you see it, ma'am?" the cop asked.

"We both did," she said.

They all turned to me. "What did you see, son?" the cop asked me.

"The red car passed us going real fast, pulled up ahead, and then just about when we couldn't see him anymore he couldn't make the turn and swerved off the road. I saw when we went by him that he was stuck in the ditch."

It felt so good to be telling the truth.

The cop went away, and the driver thanked Mum for speaking up.

It was the most exciting part of our trip home.

After three days and four nights, I saw something on the side of the road that woke me up. It was a green and white sign with a picture of a Pilgrim hat. As we got closer, I could read the words.

"Mass Pike," it said.

We were home.

Early in the afternoon the bus stopped in Milford. I didn't know why I felt nervous.

We collected our suitcases and walked down Main to South Main, to Chapin, and then to Grammy's house on

Otis Street. We were met by my sister Patty who lived on the first floor with my aunt and uncle and my two cousins Daryl and Barbara.

Patty had rented an apartment for us across town on Fayette Street. By late afternoon, we climbed up the front steps and parked our luggage in the kitchen. I sat at the wooden drop-leaf table. Just as I was about to ask if we could get something to eat, a rat ran across the floor.

"Don't unpack," my mother said. She appeared as tired as I felt.

Patty said she had found another place across town that was for rent, but she had chosen this one because it cost less.

My mother used a neighbor's phone and called the landlord. He showed up only a few minutes later.

"I'm sorry lady, but your daughter signed a lease. You can't just leave."

"Fine," my mother said. "I'll let my husband know. I think you may know him. Jack Hourihan?"

"Sure, I know Jack. You know, I guess you haven't been here long enough for me to worry about a lease, and she's only in high school, so I guess the lease isn't really binding anyways."

I guessed he did know my father.

"Good," Mum said. She held out her hand for the

return of the rent money, and then she said to us, "Get the suitcases."

We trekked back across town and began to settle into the other apartment.

"How many children are there?" the new landlord asked.

"Four," Mum answered, and he nodded.

Just as we were settled in the new place, Mum handed me a grocery list. I walked outside, and after only a few minutes walking toward Stop & Shop, it began to pour cats and dogs.

In Phoenix, when it rains you go outside and play. Here, people ducked into cars, or doorways, or hid under umbrellas. Me, I just ran, laughing, not missing any puddles. The rain soaked through my t-shirt and shorts and dripped down my face.

I felt free.

I felt like me.

I felt I was being washed.

I felt like I was finally home again.

The people who hid in doorways smiled at me as I ran by them.

I went past the bank, past the drug store, down across Central Street and past the fruit stand. The rain on the oranges, apples, and cantaloupe gave off a smell that made me slow down and enjoy it. I stood for a few minutes under the protection of the overhanging dark green awning. The beautiful, natural smell overtook me. I took a peach, ran inside and paid for it, and then, stepping back onto the street, I stood in the rain and enjoyed the fruit. Only when I was finished did I continue on past the A&P to the Stop & Shop where my sister Patty worked as a cashier.

I was soaked when I got to the market, and I slipped, fell, and covered a spot on the floor with water. Everyone in the front of the store saw me dripping all over the place just inside the doorway. A mother and her two children, on their way out of the store, smiled at me as they edged by without stepping in the water.

I waited until I wasn't dripping as much and went on into the store and bought what the list said to buy. A boy I knew from one of the older classes at St. Mary's, Francis — but everyone called him Franny — was sent to mop up the water. I knew what kind of bike he rode to school. He smiled at me. I knew his younger sister. His smile was a friendly smile of recognition rather than the one of derision I had been used to for the past year.

The rain had stopped by the time I arrived home, but I was still soaked.

I walked into our new kitchen and put the bags on the

table. I sat wet on a kitchen chair. My wet clothes made me feel something that I had missed. I felt cool, and I realized something else. I was happy.

I felt safe.

The next morning, I got up early and walked to Winter Street. I cut through the gas station on the corner and crossed to the front of the high school. This was the holiest street in Milford. I walked past the schools, the statue of St. Joseph, the convent, the rectory, and stood in front of the church.

I walked inside the front door for the first time in more than a year, then stopped. It occurred to me it was probably the first time I had, by myself, opened the church doors from the nave to the church proper. There seemed to be a soft wind blowing toward me from the direction of the altar, carrying the remnant smell of incense and palms. I felt that I was in a place I was meant to be. I stood and saw in front of me every midnight Mass, every Sunday, every holy day. I saw my ever-growing family. I felt the love for this religion I'd had from the time I was in first grade.

The main room of the church was large, four rows of pews wide, with the metal and glass gothic hanging lights, three feet long and a foot in diameter, hanging from the ceiling.

I took a deep breath and inhaled air I knew, air that had been part of my childhood. I remembered the bells ringing a deep, reverberating sound that when I was young, I heard all the way to Purchase Street. As I stepped inside the church, the bells of St. Mary's rang again. I laughed at the dramatic effect.

The church was so much bigger without people in it, and it was colder, but the comforting smell and the sunlight shining through the stained-glass windows brought back feelings of safety and belonging. Art, the painted Stations of the Cross, lined both sides, but I was riveted on the front of the church. As if looking into a perspective painting, I saw the Murphy Oil-soaped wooden pews lining both sides, getting smaller and smaller as they approached the statues of Mary and Joseph. Next I saw the rail where, during Mass, the communion goers knelt for the Eucharist. I remembered the day of my first holy communion when my hunger made my stomach growl so loud the whole church could hear me. How my friend Jake and I laughed when I found I could make it growl out loud on cue and kept doing it. Then came the gold and white of the story-high altar, and at the pinnacle of the vision, in the center, the golden tabernacle.

I took a few steps forward to a pew and sat down.

My first five years at St. Mary's ran through my mind, a welcomed memory.

I turned to the left and saw the pulpit raised fifteen feet about the parish, from where I had heard so many Sundays of, "the gospel according to…"

I smiled.

I turned around.

"Hello." The voice was unexpected. There in the back row was Sister Mary Patrick. She had entered behind me, and I never heard her footsteps or the door opening. She was kneeling when I turned and now sat back onto the rich, dark brown wooden pew.

She smiled.

An icy feeling that had been frozen in my heart a long time ago came back to me. It chilled my soul.

"Sister," I acknowledged.

I began to walk past her on my way out of the church. Visions of when she had dragged me here from the schoolyard when I was just five years old came back. She was a nun, and I knew I was supposed to respect her, and it was not difficult to respect all the other sisters of St. Joseph, but she was part of the cause of my recurring nightmare.

As I began to pass by her, she put her hand out and more gently than I thought possible of her, she placed it on my arm. She looked sadly into my eyes.

"Welcome home, John," she said, as if she had been inside my head from the second I had entered.

All I could think of was, "How can she think everything is okay?"

"Thank you, Sister," I said and left the building, walked out onto Winter Street and headed for home.

Chapter Sixteen
A Year of Confirmation
September

The return to school was pleasurable but nervous.

There were a few new students in the class, but for the most part the seats were filled with old friends who thought they knew me.

We clambered into our seats and waited for Sister to enter the room. She popped her head in and said, "I will be right back. Say an Our Father."

As most began a silent prayer, or at least made believe they were praying, Robert stood. Robert was a friend. He brushed his dark hair from his eyes with his hand and then reached into his pocket. He moved cautiously to the door through which Sister had just exited and peeked into the hall. Seeing no one, he proceeded across the room to the window that overlooked the front door and Winter Street. He went to the corner and retrieved the long pole with the hook on the end that was used to open and close the massive windows in the school. Taking a last glance over his shoulder, he opened the window.

From his pocket he took a salute, its fuse sticking an inch out of the end. He laughed. I laughed too. Was he really going to do this?

He lit the firecracker, stepped away from the window and threw it out into the air, headed for the front of the school. It didn't make it. Two things happened almost simultaneously. The first thing was the lit firecracker hit the window, bounced, and landed on the foot-wide sill, its fuse still hissing. The second thing was that Sister returned.

He was in the midst of a dilemma. Should he push it out the window, and what if it didn't make it, or should he just let it go off and take the consequence?

He decided on a third alternative.

Again my friend closed his eyes, and put his hand over the salute. It went off with a muffled pop, and he grimaced. We were that afraid of these heavenly humans, the Sisters of St. Joseph. To us, they were little old women who could kill you with a stare, or the young ones who could freeze you with a smile, and we would blow up our own hand rather than let them know we had defied them. At least I'm sure that is how Robert felt at that moment.

Sister looked at him, assessed the situation, but had no idea what had just happened. His hand had sufficiently muffled the explosion. As the entire class tried not to laugh, Sister beckoned him to her with her crooked finger, saw the burned palm of his hand, shook her head in disbelief, and sent him to the basement to take care of his wound. I believe she never knew what had happened. I think she believed it was a sign from God, sort of a salute stigmata.

Our daily lesson began.

"What is Confirmation, class?" she asked. She said the word "class" because she wanted the entire class to answer in unison. If she hadn't said the word "class" it would mean she was going to prowl the class to find someone who didn't know the answer. Nuns were extremely adept at finding the one person in the class who didn't know the answer. I believed it was a gift from God.

"Confirmation is a Sacrament through which we receive the Holy Ghost to make us strong and perfect Christians and soldiers of Jesus Christ." We all said in unison, and it sounded like the answers mumbled at Mass on Sunday by the entire congregation.

"When was confirmation instituted, class?"

"The exact time at which Confirmation was instituted is not known. But as this Sacrament was administered by the Apostles and numbered with the other Sacraments instituted by Our Lord, it is certain that He instituted this Sacrament also and instructed His Apostles in its use, at some time before His ascension into heaven."

This, of course, was a long and complicated answer, so it sounded a lot like the answers from the congregation at church, a jumble of words that made little or no sense, only spouted to show the nun in front of us that we knew the answer or at least a bunch of words that sufficed as an answer.

"Why is Confirmation so called?" She began to prowl. Then she settled on, "Jake."

"Confirmation is so called from its chief effect, which is to strengthen or render us more firm in whatever belongs to our faith and religious duties," Jake said. He was right.

"Why are we called soldiers of Jesus Christ?" She prowled again. "Mr. Hourihan."

I thought for a second or two, and just when she was about to move on, I began my answer.

"Well, when you find a wallet in a supermarket with eight hundred and fifty-six dollars in it, and a quarter, two dimes, and three pennies, and you could use the money for a new baseball glove or food, but instead you return it to the woman at the courtesy desk, I guess you are a soldier of Jesus Christ. What do you think, sister?"

"Welcome home, Mr. Hourihan." She almost laughed, but not quite.

She moved on. "Kathleen?"

"We are called soldiers of Jesus Christ to indicate how we must resist the attacks of our spiritual enemies and secure our victory over them by following and obeying Our Lord."

Sister turned back to me and smiled.

It occurred to me that the year I spent in Phoenix prepared me for Confirmation. It seemed to me that I had already spent a year of confirmation. That I had already been Confirmed.

The day was uneventful after that, except at recess.

At recess, the school driveway slipped off the road and immediately downhill between the two buildings, the red brick high school on the right and the pink granite grammar school on the left, and then down further into a tarred expanse where we played, cradled by the other building, the St. Joseph's Guild home where the mothers met at night. It was the scholarship of the St. Joseph's Guild that my sister Pat had expected to get but hadn't. It turned out that in order to get the St. Joseph's Guild scholarship, your parents had to have paid their dues. So, even though Pat had the best grades in her class, financially, she wasn't eligible. The scholarship had gone to a friend of hers.

It had been raining for three days or so and everything was soaked. It was a rain-jacket-and-hat lunch time, and we first-through-eighth-graders had huddled between the two big buildings for shelter and body heat. Recess was recess, rain or shine.

Usually those of us in the seventh grade ran around, but today it was too wet, so the hard tarred schoolyard was too slippery for worn, smooth-soled shoes to get traction. So there we mulled, me and Jake, punching each other from time to time just to keep warm.

We had a friend, Froggy Loupier, who was kind of a weird but good kid. He had a too-big head; too-big brown eyes encircled by too-big Coke-bottle glasses with a black patch over one lazy eye, a too big mouth, and his teeth stuck straight out at you when he talked.

The only thing that wasn't too big was his nose — and the rest of his body. To all of us, he was a frog with hair.

That was, of course, why everyone called him Froggy.

Froggy came running up Main Street, about fifty yards away. He crossed, sprinting through the parking lot of Zersky's gas station, and headed for the intersection with Winter Street.

The school faced Winter.

Instinctively, everyone turned to see where Sister Mary Patrick was. She was the toughest nun of the lot and said often of yard duty, "It is something to offer up for the souls in purgatory," so we knew she didn't think much of standing out here watching us.

It wouldn't do for Loupier to get caught off school property where he shouldn't be, especially not by her.

He darted across the road holding a foot-square brown paper bag. Half-way across the road, his Cub Scout hat blew off. He stopped, bent, and retrieved it in one swoop.

Mary Patrick was on the other side of the building and couldn't see him. He had reached safety when it happened. His feet started slipping, his arms flailed, and then he rose and nose-dived, flat on his face in the driveway.

It was just like him to hang onto the hat and lose touch with the bag. It sailed up then crashed to the asphalt. The contents shattered and were regurgitated from the bag in a shotgun of pieces. And they skipped across the schoolyard like stones across water. Some of the remnants slid right to my feet. It had been some kind of dinner plate, with a picture of the shattered Holy Family on it, and something had been etched on the edge in gold paint. I read it. "To The Bes…" it said on the biggest piece.

The whole yard laughed at once to see Froggy, face down, his bagged prize at the feet of various clumps of recessers.

He looked up, glasses all crooked on his big head, tears rolling down his face, and his nose running.

No human being could ever have been more vulnerable, not even naked in a dream.

He lay there flat, his head raised, eyes searching for a friendly face in a crowd of unfriendly faces.

At my feet, The Blessed Virgin Mary admonished me, and I stopped laughing.

Froggy's eyes caught mine. He was only about fifteen feet away, and he said, "I had it made special. It's my mother's birthday present." Then he returned to bawling.

I don't know what made me pick him up. It wasn't like me, and I sure don't know who said, "I'm sorry, Lenny."

As I walked away, I saw him stumble the driveway gauntlet of laughing and heckling kids. I leaned against the hard granite.

No one really saw what happened next and wouldn't have believed it of me if they had.

Jake assessed me strangely and asked, "What's wrong with your eyes?"

"It's wet out here," I said. "How long we got left?"

I couldn't have choked out another syllable, or they would have known what was going on.

It seemed Arizona hadn't changed me all that much. If nothing else, I knew for sure now that I was home.

When I returned to class, we were still being taught about Confirmation, and I read, "It is evident from its celebration that the effect of the sacrament of Confirmation is the special outpouring of the Holy Spirit as once granted to the apostles on the day of Pentecost... Recall then that you have received the spiritual seal, the spirit of wisdom and understanding, the spirit of right judgment and courage, the spirit of knowledge and reverence, the spirit of holy fear in God's presence. Guard what you have received. God the Father has marked you with his sign; Christ the Lord has confirmed you and has placed his pledge, the Spirit, in your hearts."

I thought, "And He did it all in one year."

Chapter Seventeen

Confirmed

About a month later, the rest of my family came home, and now we had seven children in the family, so we got thrown out of the new apartment.

Dennis seemed very unhappy and talks with the twins explained why.

When we had left for home, they had moved back to South Second Street for a short time, and then my father had decided it would be best to move into a trailer that he found out about while having a few beers one night. The trailer hadn't been hooked up, so there was no working bathroom, and an extension cord for electricity, but he didn't have to pay rent, and that would mean he could pay the market sooner and save enough to move home sooner. The trailer was left sitting behind a bar, probably where he found out about it. In order to go to the bathroom, my sisters and brother had to use the one in the house behind the bar where the people who owned the trailer lived. The woman didn't like them using her bathroom, and she didn't always say yes.

One such night when Dennis had to go to the bathroom, Nancy had taken him to the house to ask the women to let them in.

The woman stood at the door and shouted, "You used the one in the trailer last night, didn't you?"

"No," Nancy said.

"You liar, I saw it. Someone peed, and it ran out all over the ground under the trailer." The woman had continued her tirade, but Nancy took Dennis by the hand and said, "Come on Dennis, we don't have to listen to this. We're done." They walked into the trailer and used the bathroom.

Their lives for about a month were worse than anything the rest of us had experienced in our year-long visit to Arizona.

As soon as we were told to leave our apartment in Milford, my father talked his distant cousin into allowing us to rent the third story of his house on Winter Street, only a few houses away from the church. It was as if we had moved to heaven. I went to Mass almost every day.

I also found out something about the usefulness of being a cute little Catholic boy from St. Mary's. I had reconnected with Pudge, and we devised a plan to get a View Master without raising the money to pay for it. I told him I would create a diversion so the woman clerk at Woolworth's five and dime would be focused only on me, and he could grab the View Master, tuck it under his coat, and leave the store. I went home and got out a carrot and a potato peeler. With the peeler, I sliced off a very thin, almost translucent slice of carrot. When we entered the store, Pudge went directly to the toy section. I went to the fish tanks where guppies and gold fish lived. When I saw that Pudge was at his station, I coughed so the woman would turn in my direction. When she did, I plunged my hand with the carrot slice into the fish tank, pulled it out, and wiggling the carrot slice, I popped it into my mouth. For all the world, it was as if I had just eaten a goldfish.

Pudge was laughing so hard he forgot to steal the View Master. The woman came to me and asked me if I was hungry. I erupted in laughter, turned, and ran. She must have thought I was insane.

The next day, we tried another store, Grant's, and I

found that when you are carrying a dark green school bag with the St. Mary's emblem on it nobody expected you would have lined it with a piece of cardboard to keep the empty school bag open inside, and then fill it with, among other things, a View Master.

That afternoon, I sat on my bed with the day's take spread out. I could see the church out my window. The bells rang. I pulled everything together and stuffed it into my school bag.

I trekked the half mile or so down Main Street, walked into Grant's, took the escalator down into the toy section, and put everything back. It felt good.

Instead of going home, I went to the Worcester Telegram office and got a paper route. I figured I was home, and I should at least try to be who I wanted to be before my family had left for Arizona.

When I got to the house, Diane was getting ready for a date. Something occurred to me. I went to my bureau and reached under the socks and t-shirts and took out something I had rescued from my home on Purchase Street long ago.

I carried it with me to the kitchen. Sheila was on the phone, so I waited.

After a short time, she glared at me, covered the mouthpiece and said, "What?"

"I want to use the phone," I said.

She squinted at me and must have been thinking, "Who the hell would he be calling?"

At twelve, I never used the phone for anything but calling a cab for my mother, and since it was getting dark, she must have figured I wasn't doing that.

Eventually she got off the phone.

I had looked up the number while she was talking, and now I dialed.

"Hello?"

"Hello, can I speak with Lorraine?"

The adult voice on the other end of the line sounded confused, but she said okay, and in only a few seconds, an equally confused Lorraine answered.

"Yes?"

"Hi, Lorraine, It's John Hourihan. I was wondering if you would like to go to a movie with me Saturday."

There was silence for a few confused seconds, and then she said, "Yes, okay."

"Good," I said. "I'll meet you at your house around noon. There's a show at one. We can walk."

"Okay," she said and hung up.

As I hung up, my sisters, who had been standing in the kitchen watching, cheered.

"Very well done," Diane said.

The phone rang, and I answered it.

"Hello?"

"Is this John?"

"Yes."

"I'm sorry. My father says I'm too young to date. Maybe next year, he said."

"Oh. Okay." I hung up.

My class had our confirmation in the eighth grade rather than waiting for high school, because too many out-of-towners would be coming into the school in the ninth grade. The school must have been worried that, since the newcomers wouldn't have attended St. Mary's, they would not have had the concentrated instruction our class had had since we were five or six years old, and a nun stood in front of us and asked, "Who is God, class?"

A meeting of the nuns and priests took place at the St. Joseph's Guild building. Since I had spent my sixth grade at a non-parochial school, whether or not I should be confirmed with my class was still to be decided. I wasn't at the meeting, but I was told a week or so later in class that I would be allowed to go ahead with my classmates and be confirmed.

I thanked Sister when she told me, but I didn't understand why it was a problem at all, or why I should be thanking anyone.

That night I called Lorraine again and was told, "Not yet."

On that perfectly sunny day, we stood in front of the church on Winter Street that had been blocked off to traffic. We all believed now that we knew who God was. After some prayers, we lined up to kiss the ring of the Bishop and become religious soldiers. Standing in that line, I realized I had received from the Holy Ghost most of my knowledge, understanding, wisdom, counsel, fortitude, piety and fear of the Lord not here, but during my year away from the church in a barrio, in the desert, in South Phoenix.

I walked up to the man in the robes standing in front of my class, then I knelt, bent over, put my hand over the ring and kissed my own hand. The Bishop noticed but wasn't sure what had just happened, so he said nothing.

As I began my exit, I saw the sun blinking at me from just behind the church tower, so I winked back at God.

Chapter Eighteen
Hell in a Hand Basket

I believed in this religion. It seemed to keep me doing, or at least wanting to do, things that the purveyors of the doctrine told me were the right things to do. I kept screwing it up, but I kept trying. That was my spiritual self, but there was also reality. There was faith, hope, and charity, but there was also hunger, pain, and fear.

My brother was sick, through no one's fault, and my family had been torn to pieces trying to save the one child by moving the entire family to a barrio in the desert, or maybe it was for a different reason.

When the ceremony in front of the church was over, I only had a short walk to my current home.

I pulled an aluminum patio chair out of the barn and

sat on it on the small lawn beside the house. Where I was sitting had a nice view of Mr. Sullivan's garden and beyond it, the church.

Arizona came back to me; the stifling heat, the huge division between the very rich and the very poor. I thought of the boss in the cotton field not wanting to pay me for my work so he could save seventy-five cents, and the Mexican family who was going home in a truck after a long day in the field. I remembered for a few seconds that Mexican children and Irish children smelled the same when we sweated. I thought of my sister Diane being forced to be a mother at fifteen and what it had done to her, and the way she stepped in and stopped a rape. I pictured that innocent cow being butchered so we could eat and so we could be entertained, and I saw the bull chasing Freddie because he had stuck up for his little cousin.

I wasn't so sure anymore that this religion did anything for poor people, even though it seemed to be the poor who kept trying to go by the rules. Adults couldn't be the answer, I figured, since Crazy Willie's old man nearly knocked Nancy and me over trying to get out of that burning house, and my own father's ego nearly got himself killed while he was the sole support of his three kids sitting in a Quonset hut waiting for him to come home from work. My coaches had proven to me that I was just someone who could get them to "the TV game," and Duke was a moron who nearly killed us all coming down South Mountain, and again when he thought it was a great idea to toss me in the irrigation canal to teach me to swim.

For the past year, my life had felt like it did while crawling out over that dam in the pitch black night with the hope that each step would be the right one, and we would return to the shore alive.

I thought of Ross and Johna-Jean and the way we kids took care of what everyone else would have messed up. I had had a knife fight at eleven years old, and no one even batted an eye, and I was playing with scorpions as if they were so many grasshoppers. And at the end of a gang fight, the only thing that happened was we got to play wherever we wanted. I also started counting, and I figured out I was twelve years old, and, in my life, my family had moved ten times. I chalked it up to being Irish. Gram always said the Irish were nomads. "Iberia to Hibernia," she used to say. I had no idea what it meant.

I heard a noise and turned to see my mother carrying the other aluminum chair and two glasses of iced tea. She sat the chair down beside me, handed me a tea, and sat down.

"So, you made your Confirmation, Mr. John Thomas Francis Hourihan. How does it feel?"

"I want to transfer to Milford High School," I said.

"Why?"

"The rules here aren't making sense to me."

"Like what?"

"The Ten Commandments, for one thing."

She drank and thought. "I guess you're right. They are pretty hard to go by."

"And this Confirmation," I said. "I'm old enough now to be, what did they call it, a soldier for Jesus Christ, but I'm not old enough to go to a movie with a girl? That makes no sense."

"She said, no, huh?"

"No," I blurted. "She said yes. Her idiot father said no."

"Oh." She smiled. "Maybe next year."

"That's what he said."

"So you don't like the rules? Too hard?"

I sat for a while then said, "No. I like the rules, kind of. I just still don't think anyone goes by them. Why do I have to learn them if no one else believes in them?"

"Like what?" she asked.

It was comforting to be having this conversation with my mother and to have her not blindly say I had to go by the rules and shut up.

"Okay," I said. "Thou shalt not kill. We kill everyone. God even told us to kill everyone. It makes no sense to say 'kill everyone' and then say 'thou shalt not kill'. And steal?"

"I think you may be breaking that one a bit," she said and smiled.

I winced. "I brought everything back," I said.

"Good. What else?"

"Lies?" I looked at her and wondered if I dared ask. So I did. "Did we really go to Arizona because of Dennis?"

"Some," she answered. "And some to get your father a job. He was having trouble getting one here."

"Come on Mum. No one actually obeys these commandments, and sometimes I don't think they are right. Do you think Garrett and Posey should have honored their father? The man is a fool. He damn near got us killed, more than once. And maybe someone should tell Denny it wasn't all his fault that we had to move to a desert."

"So you want to just give up on the religion thing, because of Duke?" she asked.

"Maybe," I said. "And this Confirmation thing. The school thinks the kids who spent last year at St. Mary's are more ready to be soldiers of Jesus than someone like me who spent the past year learning about real stuff and trying to understand it, not like reading it in the Baltimore Catechism."

"Like what?" Mum asked.

I thought for a few seconds. "Like who understands fear of the Lord better than I do after coming down South Mountain at 60? And all the rest, I mean, I lived all those things: piety, fortitude, all of them. The kids here learned it in a book. It's not the same, but they had 'to decide' if I knew enough to be confirmed with my class."

"I understand," Mum said. "If you never face the dangers, how do you know if you are going to be a good soldier?"

"Right." I couldn't have said it myself, but I recognized it as what I meant.

"So the rules are hard, or no one goes by them, so you just feel you should give up on them? You don't think a human being can go by them?"

"I don't," I said.

"Me neither," she said.

I never could hit a curve, I thought.

"You don't believe we can go by them either?" I asked. I was stunned.

"Nope. Someone told me once that even though the rules are hard, and we can't go by them all the time, at least we have to try. This person told me you'd have to be

God to do it right all the time. Is anyone punishing you for trying but not getting it right?"

I thought for a while. "No, I guess not."

"Okay," Mum said. "I was told by this person that other people shouldn't be in charge of us."

"That was me, right?" I said. "I told you that, back in first grade, after the stuff at the church. The exorcism."

"Yes, it was you, and you said that you, me and God are the ones you would answer to."

She stood up, handed me her tea glass, folded the chair and said, "Don't worry Johnny, as long as you keep trying, you aren't going to hell in a hand basket." She smiled and started walking toward the house.

I guess the book and the nuns were right.

It had been a hell of a year, but I was finally confirmed.

Before we reached the back door, she turned around as if she had only just decided something.

"And don't be so quick about going to Milford High School. We may be moving again soon."

Coming Soon:

Baltimore Catechism: The Mass of the Faithful

I figured out early in life that it is best to learn the rules before you try to play the game. Parochial grammar school taught me some rules I was supposed to go by. The Sisters of the order of St. Joseph taught the laws of the Baltimore Catechism, augmented by my sainted grandmother Rose Briget O'Flynn Hourihan herself. Now, I was to be tossed into the secular humanism of public high school where I would get to profess my faith in those rules… or not.

Public high school was about to teach me that knowing the rules, and trying to go by them, only works when they are good rules. I also found out that most rules of law and religion are made by men with very earthly agendas fitting their own prejudices.

I learned that, no matter what I promised my mother, I was still just "an Irish punk from Milford" in the eyes of the some of the people in the White Anglo Saxon Protestant town of Hopedale.

About the Author

John T. Hourihan Jr., a retired journalist, has won state, regional and national awards for his opinion column in several New England newspapers. He received the Cross of Gallantry for valor in Vietnam, where he served three tours as a Vietnamese linguist. He is disabled now from the effects of Agent Orange. He lives with his author wife Lin Hourihan (*The Virtue of Virtues*, *The Mystery of the Sturbridge Keys*) in the woods of central Massachusetts. His other works include *Baltimore Catechism: Clean Slate*; *The Mustard Seed – 2095*, *The Mustard Seed – 2110*, *The Mustard Seed – 2130*, *Beyond the Fence: Converging Memoirs*, *Parables for a New Age I and II*, *Play Fair and Win*.